THE STORY OF THE SQUAW

The Story of the Squaw
A Lucas Penny Book
Book 1
By Jared McVay

Published by Creative Texts Publishers, LLC
PO Box 50
Barto, PA 19504
www.creativetexts.com

ISBN: 978-1-64738-055-7

THE STORY OF THE SQUAW

A LUCAS PENNY BOOK

BOOK 1

by

Jared McVay

"To survive, a man must be willing to die…"

- an unknown mountain man

Table of Contents

ONE

Stares at the Moon sat, huddled in his blankets, glaring at the small fire that was fighting to warm his makeshift shelter. The smoke wasn't dissipating through the hole at the top like it should and the interior was filling up with smoke. He had no buffalo robes to make a proper teepee and had been forced to make a place to get in out of the storm, from whatever pieces of wood and brush he could find which was far from ideal as far as he was concerned.

He was seized with rage. His chattering teeth could hardly get out the words, "The white man must die. I will see him skinned alive – a little at a time – then I will bury him up to his neck near an ant hill, and cover his head with honey."

The thought of the punishment he would inflict on the white man calmed him somewhat and he pulled back the covering of the doorway to let out some of the smoke, then added more wood to the fire and bundled up in his blankets, again, the bruises on his body making it difficult for him to get comfortable.

He eased his body down close to the fire to get as much warmth as he could, and tried to sleep. But sleep was not to be had. He was cold, but that was not what was keeping him awake. Every time he closed his eyes, he saw Crying Dove in his mind – and she was laughing at him.

Outside, the winter storm, high in the Colorado mountains, continued to rage, covering the ground with large snowflakes. The wind tore its way through every opening it could find in the makeshift hut. The only redeeming factor was that the depth of the snow was closing a good many of the hut's cracks. He looked at the opening doorway and saw the snow was already covering half of the opening. He could only hope the weight of the snow wouldn't cause the flimsy hut to cave in.

He knew if the storm continued - by morning, he would be completely snowed in and would have to dig a hole to the surface so he would have air to breathe. He laughed. The smoke imprisoned inside the hut would probably suffocate him first.

His stomach began to growl and he sat up. He hadn't eaten in two days and his stomach was not happy about it. Stares at the Moon filled a hollow gourd with snow, then held it over the small fire and allowed it to melt. At least he would have water to drink.

As he sipped the melted snow, he wondered where the white man and Crying Dove were? Were they warm and dry in some cabin built by the white man – eating food and laughing at him? Just the thought of them together caused his anger to rise once more.

This was Stares at the Moon's twenty-fourth winter and as he looked back, he realized the mistakes he had made.

He had been born on the plains, many miles south of where he now was. As a young boy, the mountains, had always looked mysterious and beautiful, had always looked so appealing, but they were deceiving. While there were rivers and trees and animals of many descriptions, the weather was much harsher and the land unforgiving. There were gullies so steep and hills so rugged, a man struggled to go on foot. Taking a horse was out of the question. A man must learn to go around to find his destination. On the plains, a man could ride his horse forever, and there were buffalo as far as the eye could see - whose hide made warm teepees, and the meat filled the bellies of his people.

As a boy he had played war games with his brethren and later, when he was older - invited to hunt the buffalo! Oh, the joy of riding at full speed - racing next to those monstrous animals – the sound of their hooves pounding on the ground, filling the sky with the sound of their running. And the young girls smiling at him shyly, giggling and talking about him because he had brought down the largest of the kill. Yes, there were elk, deer and bear in the mountains, along with deadly wolves and other animals, but they were nothing compared to a herd of stampeding buffalo.

Stares at the Moon added more wood to his meager fire, then lay back down, allowing his mind to remember better days.

On his twentieth summer a small band of Arapahoe had ventured into their territory and his uncle, Rides Tall, who was chief of the Sioux, decided to teach them a lesson for trespassing into Sioux territory, by raiding their camp and stealing all of their horses.

After much pleading, Stares at the Moon was allowed to go on the raid.

He could see it in his mind. The moon was full and bright. The sky was filled with stars and excitement filled the air like static from a lightning strike. They were riding in at high speed, yelling and screaming creating fear in the hearts of the weakling, Arapahoe.

On the night of the raid, instead of riding in like Stares at the Moon had dreamed about, they crept up close to where the horses were kept and saw only one brave guarding them. He and Chases Dogs were told to overpower the brave guarding the horses. "But do not kill him," Rides Tall, told them.

Filled with pride at being chosen, he and Chases Dogs crawled on their stomachs to within a few feet of the guard and waited for the right moment to pounce on him.

But just before the moment came, Stares at the Moon saw something in the corner of his eye that made him look away. A beautiful, young squaw, had gone down to the small nearby creek and he watched as she took off her clothes and waded into the water. He was mesmerized and no longer had any thoughts about what he was there to do.

Chases Dogs whispered, "Now!" and leaped up and ran toward the guard, but instead of following Chases Dogs, Stares at the Moon jumped up and ran toward the creek where the young woman was bathing in the water. And when he got there, he saw the young woman stop her bathing when she heard the sound of the horses being stampeded.

Stares at the Moon grabbed her buckskin dress from the limb it was hanging on and stepped behind a tree.

When she came out of the creek and ran to where she'd left her clothes, Stares at the Moon swallowed hard. Water glistened off her young, ripe body and at that moment, she was the most beautiful woman he'd ever seen. But to be truthful, she was the first woman he'd ever seen without any clothes.

When she got close, Stares at the Moon stepped out and grabbed her, putting his knife to her throat. "Stay silent or you will die!" he whispered.

Although she did not understand what the brave said, the knife against her throat told her all she needed to know and she stood quietly, watching as her people's horses were driven right through the center of the village. There was a lot of shouting and gunfire. People were running in all directions, trying not to get run down by the horses, but not all of them made it, which made Rides Tall, angry because this raid was only to steal horses, not kill anyone.

Stares at the Moon allowed her to get dressed, then shoved her in the opposite direction of all the excitement. A short distance away, she found herself standing next to a pinto horse. When he motioned for her to climb onto the horse, she refused and for that, she got a knife prick in the ribs. She climbed onto the horse and had planned to kick it in the ribs to make it run away, but the brave was too fast and was seated behind her before she could do anything.

Almost three hours later, not far ahead of the rising sun, they came into the Sioux village and he herded her into a teepee, where he tried to have his way with her, but she fought like a she-wolf protecting her cubs, and

7

he finally gave up, but not before she was beaten so bad her eyes were almost swollen shut and her nose bled down onto her chest. Her ribcage was black and blue and it was hard to breathe. But she had remained the fair maiden she had been before being kidnapped.

She was afraid to go to sleep and was lying there on the blankets he'd provided when three men entered the teepee and kicked Stares at the Moon in the back, forcing him to his feet.

She had no idea who the men were, but she believed they were the chief and two elders. At least that's the way it worked in her tribe when someone was in trouble.

One of the men, the older of the three, was shouting at the brave and at one point, pointed at her and then slapped the brave, knocking him to his knees.

The look he had in his eyes was enough to frighten even the dead – but he stood up, gritting his teeth, but saying nothing. The man she guessed was the chief, pointed at her, again, and said something.

The young brave glared at the man, but nodded his head, up and down.

What she didn't know was, the chief was very angry that Stares at the Moon had not gone with Chases Dogs to stampede the horses as he had been instructed to do and Chases Dogs was nearly killed in his struggle to overpower the guard – and now lay at death's door.

As far as Rides Tall and the two elders were concerned, it was Stares at the Moon's fault. Plus, he had stolen a young squaw – and that had not been part of the plan. The chief had called him a disgrace to the tribe and ordered him to return the horses and the squaw back to the Arapahoe.

Stares at the Moon recalled wondering what the Arapahoe would have done to him – knowing his people would not care, or interfere.

Thinking quickly, Stares at the Moon agreed to do as the chief said, and as soon as Rides Tall and the elders left, he began packing.

He didn't have much time before the sun came up and then it would be too late. Within fifteen minutes, he had a small bag packed and had gagged the woman and herded her out to the area where the horses were grazing peacefully.

He owned only one horse, but his plan called for two. He looked over his shoulder at the silent camp and whispered, "You are no longer my people and as an outsider, it is within my right to steal a horse from you."

And with that, he tied his few possessions on the back of a sorrel mare, one he had had an eye on for some time, then forced the young squaw onto the horse's back, tying her feet to the underside of the belly of the horse. Leading both his horse and the stolen one, he sneaked off into the early morning haze.

Half a mile from the camp, he mounted his horse and headed north into the far distant mountains – a place he doubted they would follow.

Stares at the Moon sat up and refilled his gourd with snow, then held it over the meager fire.

As he sipped the melted snow, he remembered the trip into the mountains. His hope and desire the young squaw would one day, relent to become his woman, had never materialized. She refused to speak to him and cooked only so she could eat, too. And when he tried to mate with her, she fought like a female animal out of season. Even when he beat her, still, she fought.

"What is wrong with you woman?" he remembered shouting at her. "Am I not a good-looking warrior? Do you not find me favorable?"

All he got was a glare and bared teeth. He had to tie her at night for fear she would try to run away or even worse, try to kill him while he slept.

He convinced himself that once they were high up into the mountains where he could find a place to make a proper camp, she would come around. And if not, he would beat her into submission. One way or another, she would be his woman.

Weariness and lack of food was finally catching up to Stares at the Moon and his eyes began to droop. The gourd slipped from his hand and he fell over, oblivious to the raging storm outside.

TWO

Lucas Penny struggled to wade through the ever-deepening snow. It was nearly knee-deep and would have been hard going by himself, but with a young Indian squaw on his back, it was all he could do to move one foot in front of the other. He could hear her labored breathing and feel her arms and legs clinging tightly to him.

The freezing wind had increased. It was driving into his face making it hard to breathe and the snow was falling heavier now - and he still had at least two miles to go before reaching his cabin. He looked to his left, then his right, but there was no shelter, even in among the trees. He had no choice but to keep moving.

The young woman made a groaning noise, which increased Lucas' resolve to keep going.

As he struggled on, his mind went back to when he'd first come up on the young woman and the brave who was beating and kicking her. Even though she was trying to fight back, the brave was much bigger and stronger and she was losing the battle.

Lucas had been out hunting for meat to see him through the storm he saw coming in from the north. He could sense it would be a big one that could last for several weeks. He had enough supplies and firewood to last out a storm, but he needed meat.

He was a good five miles from his cabin and had yet to see any deer or elk, which was what he was searching for. The wind had picked up some, and the snow was just beginning to fall when he heard the scream of a woman's voice as it radiated through the trees.

Lucas ran toward the sound, but hauled up short when he saw the camp and the battle going on between a young woman and an Indian brave.

Before rushing into the scene, he stepped behind a tree to observe – and what he saw made the hackles on the back of his neck, rise. She was a young, Indian squaw. He knew Indian men beat their women to show their power over them, but what Lucas couldn't understand was, why would a man, twice as large as the woman he was beating on, think he needed to beat and kick a woman to get her to do as he wanted? It made no sense. He knew from experience that didn't work.

His father had been a hard-headed man, who abused everyone, even his mother, and when he came home in one of his drunken rages, she did her best to hide from him. When he couldn't find her to beat on, he turned to his son. From the time Lucas could remember, his father had taken his frustrations and anger out on him. He would come home, half in his cups, looking for Lucas' mother, and when he couldn't find her, still filled with anger, he would beat on Lucas until he wore himself out. Once he was passed out and peace once more came to the house, his mother would come out of hiding and hold him, crying and telling him how sorry she was.

At the ripe old age of twelve, his father took him out of school and put him to work at the cotton mill he owned. Scotland was big on sheep and the cotton mill brought in a small fortune, but to hear his father tell it, the cost of labor and overhead were driving him into the poorhouse – which wasn't true. He was just a greedy, miserly man who hated sharing any of his wealth. During those years Lucas worked at the mill, doing whatever was expected of him, without pay. And if anything went wrong, he was a prime target of his father's anger. No matter what happened, it was Lucas' fault and his father would deduct the cost from Lucas' non-existent pay to show the ones who were being paid, that he would do the same to them if they got out of line. In the end, Lucas wound up working with no pay, but receiving lots of abuse. Little by little, the resentment against his father festered and grew inside him like a tropical storm building up – ready to unleash itself with all its fury. The excuses his mother made for her husband, no longer pacified Lucas and he became broody and sullen.

On his eighteenth birthday, Lucas had had enough and decided to leave the cotton mill, his home, the abuse – all of it. At breakfast, he dropped the information on his parents and his father went crazy. He jumped to his feet and began yelling at Lucas, calling him a worthless, unappreciative lout, plus a lot of other names - then came at him with both fists doubled up. "You will not be leaving, you no-good pup! I'll show you who's the boss around here!"

Lucas jumped to his feet and yelled, "No more!"

Away from work, Lucas had built the reputation of a young man you didn't want to fight with. In fact, he'd acquired the nickname, "Bruiser." Several men older than Lucas claimed what he lacked in size, he made up for with speed and hard punching. So far, no-one in his home town had bested him in a knockdown, drag away.

So, when his father hit him alongside his head, knocking him to the floor, Lucas came to his feet and said, "Don't ever try that, ever again, old man."

His father looked at him and grinned. "So, the young pup wants to challenge the lead dog, does he? Well now, that's just fine with me. Come on, boy, let's see what you got?"

When Lucas' mother tried to step in and stop the fight, her husband backhanded her in the mouth and she was knocked to the floor. Blood began to run over her lips and stain her apron - which took Lucas over the top with anger.

He drove a left to his father's jaw, followed by a right to his stomach, causing his father to double over.

But if Lucas thought that would be the end of it, he had a rude awakening coming. His father stood up and said, "If that's all you got, boy, this ain't gonna be much of a fight."

And with that, he drove his right fist into Lucas' face, breaking his nose.

Lucas stepped back and felt the blood rushing from his nostrils and staining his shirt. He looked at his father, and laughed. Any and all restraints about standing up to his father disappeared like a puff of smoke. "All my life I thought you were tough and I was afraid of you - but the truth is, you're only tough when you're fighting with a woman or someone smaller than you. Well, I'm no longer smaller than you, old man. So, before I leave, I'm going to show you what it feels like to be beaten on."

His father was filled with rage and rushed Lucas, swinging both fists, but Lucas stepped to the side and drove his right fist into his father's stomach, again. And when his father turned to face him, Lucas was right there, pounding his father with lefts and rights, driving him backward.

His father tried to fight back but his feeble blows only urged Lucas on.

Seeing he had the advantage; Lucas drove a hard right to his father's jaw and watched as he was driven backward. Lucas was ready to follow him with more blows, but then the unexpected happened. His father lost his balance and went over backwards, knocking the fireplace shovel stand over – and when he went down, the handle of the shovel drove its way into his father's back and out through his chest.

His mother ran up next to Lucas and took ahold of his arm, saying, "That wasn't your fault. It was an accident, pure and simple."

But when the policeman arrived, he didn't see it that way. "Looks to me like the boy had a vendetta to settle with his father and saw him dead before he would quit beating on him."

He looked at Lucas' mother and said, "You know the boy has a reputation for beating up men several years older than him, don't ya? They call him, The Bruiser, because of the damage he does to his victims. Beats them nearly ta death, he does, but always inside the law. But this time he's gone too far, and I'm gonna see him prison bound."

Lucas' mother was unaware of this and said so. "You must be mistaken; Lucas is a good boy. Hard working he is. He's no troublemaker."

"Aww, the blind eye of the mother," the policeman said.

The policeman turned to Lucas and said, "Turn around boy and put your hands behind your back so's I can put the cuffs on you. And I want no trouble from you!"

Lucas stared at the policeman, and said, "It was an accident. He was in one of his rages and knocked ma down. You can see her bloody mouth. Then came at me and I was just defending myself. During our scuffle, I hit him and knocked him backward. He lost his balance and fell on the shovel. An accident, for sure. I never wanted him dead, just to know what it was like to be beaten on. That's all."

"That'll be for the judge to decide. Now, turn around and put your hands behind your back!" And with that, the policeman pulled his pistol and pointed it at Lucas. "Don't make me shoot you right here in front of your mother."

Lucas had no intention of being put in jail where who knew what could happen? With the reputation he'd gained, he would be convicted of murder and sent to the gallows where he would be publicly hanged.

He gave a sigh and shrugged his shoulders as though he was giving up, but when he turned his back to the policeman, instead of stopping, he continued on around, driving his fist into the man's jaw, dropping him to the floor, where he hit his head on the edge of a table. Blood was running onto the rug.

Lucas looked at his mother and said, "I'm sorry, ma, I didn't mean for that to happen, but I won't be put behind bars for what happened to pa. But as sure as the sun comes up in the east, he deserved it, if anyone did. You know that, doncha?"

His mother could only shake her head in agreement. And when Lucas took her in his arms for the last time, she said, "Get your bag son, then come back here."

Lucas looked down at the policeman and knew he too, was dead. He would be charged with two murders. He had no choice but to run away - so he ran to his room where he had a bag already packed, then hurried back into the living room to tell his mother goodbye. She was standing there, waiting – tears running down her face, dripping off her chin.

She pressed a wad of bills into his shirt pocket and said, "It isn't much but maybe it will be enough to get you away from here."

"Ma, I can't take…"

She took his face in her hands and kissed him, then said, "Shh, not a word about it. I own the mill, now, so I'll be fine. Now go! I'll give you an hour before I call to report what happened. I'll even say the officer attacked you. Now please, go!"

That had been twenty years back and a lot of things had happened during that time. He'd roamed throughout England, France, Portugal, and Spain, for five years, doing odd jobs, staying one step ahead of the police. He was a wanted man. He was working on the docks in Spain when his opportunity to work on a ship going to America came about and he took it.

Once he was in America, he worked his way to the mountains of Colorado where he could disappear into the high country. He'd heard about mountain men, as far back as the time he spent in South Carolina.

It was tough at first. Becoming a mountain man took much more than he'd realized from reading the dime novels. As luck would have it, on his second day out of Denver, he happened onto a fight between a mountain man and six Indians who wanted his scalp.

Without giving it any thought, he brought his rifle to bear and quickly ran the Indians off.

The man's name, he learned, was John Wesley Powell – a man who'd made a name for himself in the mountains of Colorado. And for the next three years, he learned to hunt, trap, and trade with this man, taking in every bit of knowledge he could. Seven years ago, Lucas had struck out on his own and during that time, he had made a name of his own as a mountain man to be reckoned with.

And now, he stood, looking at the Indian brave, beating on a woman half his size.

With anger welling up inside him, he dropped the pack from his back and ran toward the Indian brave, screaming like a wounded bear.

The brave turned just in time to catch a fist driven into the side of his head, causing lights to flash on and off in his head – but he was far from being beaten. He gained his balance and stared at the man in front of him. He was much smaller than him and from the look of him, he was a mountain man. He had hair down to his shoulders and a thick beard. He was dressed in buckskin clothes and wore a fur hat. Stares at the Moon had not seen many mountain men, but enough to recognize one when he saw him.

For close to half an hour, they grappled and fought – but finally, a blow to Stares at the Moon's head, almost sent him into darkness, and the mountain man took advantage of the situation. Stares at the Moon was beaten until he was not much more than a bloody pulp. And when he finally regained consciousness, his kidnapped squaw and the man, were gone.

THREE

With the storm and the weight of the woman on his back, Lucas Penny was almost all in, and he stopped to catch his breath – which turned out to be a bad idea. Snow had built up on the limb above Lucas' head and the weight caused the limb to bend, sending a large portion of snow down on the heads of Lucas and the woman.

"Dammit!" Lucas yelled as he reacted to snow going down the neck of his coat. The woman jumped and almost choked him trying to stay on his back.

After prying her hands from his throat, he lowered her to the ground and looked at her. Her face was swollen and bruised, but she was able to see through the puffiness of her cheeks. He held her arms for a few moments, allowing her to get her balance.

"Can you stand on your own?" he asked.

She stood for a moment, then nodded her head, yes.

"You understand English?" He asked.

Again, she nodded her head, yes.

"Do you speak the whiteman's language?" he ventured.

Once again, she only nodded her head, yes.

Lucas looked at her and decided she would talk when she got ready. "Do you think you can walk?"

She thought for a moment, then took a tentative step – then another. Through her swollen lips, she smiled, slightly, and nodded her head, yes.

So, with Lucas in the lead and a piece of rope tied between them so he would know if she faltered, they headed up the mountain.

A little over two hours later, Lucas stopped and pointed. "My cabin is just beyond that next rise," he told her. "Maybe less than another hour. Think you can make it?"

She nodded her head, yes and gestured for Lucas to continue on.

What sun there was to be seen, was slipping behind the trees as Lucas cleared the snow away so he could open the door to his cabin.

The inside was not warm, but not freezing cold, either. The fire he'd built before leaving on his hunting trip had burned down to nothing but red, coals. Lucas quickly added more wood to the fireplace and looked at the woman, who stood, looking around at the interior of the cabin.

In reality, it was cleaner and better equipped than most mountain man cabins. His mother had been fastidious in her housekeeping and it had rubbed off on Lucas. He liked being clean – which meant he also, bathed more often than most of the mountain men.

"It's not a palace, but it will do," Lucas told her as he made a pot of coffee and hung it over the fire to perk.

"Sit down," he told her, pointing to one of the homemade chairs sitting next to a homemade table. "I'll see to putting some medicine on your wounds, then fix us something to eat," Lucas said with a smile.

Without any shame, she stripped off her clothes and stood, naked, while Lucas washed off the blood, then applied salve to her wounds.

When he'd finished, she got dressed and sat down at the table, and to his surprise, she said, "Thank you."

Lucas grinned and said, "You are welcome. My name is Lucas Penny. What is yours?"

She smiled and said, "Because of the sadness people say I have in my eyes, I am called, Crying Dove."

Lucas didn't think they looked sad, at all. In fact, he thought she had beautiful eyes.

Over a meal of canned vegetables and what little meat he had, Lucas heard the whole story and he shook his head.

"You can rest assured, as long as I can draw breath, he will not harm you again. And when the weather clears, I will take you back to your people."

Crying Dove stared at this strange white man, who now owned her, and wanted nothing from her - except for her to get well so he could return her to her people. This white man was nothing like the stories she'd heard about white men and how they treated squaws.

She found herself blushing as she looked at him and realized he was a good-looking man, and she was having thoughts she shouldn't be having. She had never been with a man, and wasn't quite sure what to expect. She sighed, knowing he would more than likely not be her first, which caused her to have mixed feelings.

That night, he gave her the only bed in the cabin and made a pallet on the floor for himself.

When morning came, he found Crying Dove fast asleep against his back and liked the feeling. Even with all her bruises and swelling, she was a beautiful young woman and it took a lot of effort and willpower for him to move away from her.

He got to his feet and cleaned the ashes from the fireplace, then built up a fire, and hung the coffee pot over the flames to perk. He had come to like coffee, more than tea, although, sometimes in the evening, a cup of hot tea was very soothing.

He had six bird eggs on the shelf and added them to the potatoes and deer meat he would be frying for breakfast.

While the food was still cooking, Crying Dove got to her feet and left the cabin to take care of her needs.

When she returned, she asked, "Is there anything I can do?"

Lucas looked at her. She had apparently washed her face with snow and her hair was in one, long, ponytail. She was definitely a thing of beauty. "Do you know how to cook a white man's meal?"

She looked down at the floor and shook her head, no. "I went to the school at the mission, but they never taught us to cook – just how to read, write and do sums."

"But you like the tase of the white man's food? Yes?"

"Oh yes," she replied.

The coffee was ready and he poured them both a cup.

When breakfast was finished, Crying Dove insisted on cleaning up and Lucas was surprised at how thorough she was.

Lucas filled a briar pipe and sat down to write in his journal. He'd just finished with his entry when Crying Dove approached him.

"Do you think he will come for me?" she asked.

Lucas thought for a moment, then nodded his head. "Yes. He will come. He has been humiliated and from what I know of Indians, he will want my hide hanging from the wall of his teepee. And of course, he will want you back."

"But you will not give me back to him. You promised," she said with fear in her eyes.

Lucas looked at the sadness on her face and said, "I have given you my word and Lucas Penny does not go back on his word."

"When do you think he will come?" she asked

"When the snow melts enough for him to travel," Lucas told her.

She smiled. That would be some time from now, which also meant he could not take her back to her people, either.

Maybe it will be time enough to change his mind, she thought to herself as she busied herself cleaning the inside of the cabin.

Lucas watched her work and wondered what it would be like to have her here all the time?

FOUR

Stares at the Moon paced back and forth inside his hut. He had been fortunate that a deer had been trying to find shelter and found itself belly deep in the snow, just a few feet from Stares at the Moon's makeshift shelter.

Stares at the Moon had heard its crying and felt new energy flowing through him as he waded out into the snow and took what the gods had brought him. It was a sign that he would survive and be able to seek his revenge on the white man and the squaw.

Stares at the Moon walked to the opening of his hut and looked out. It had been nearly a full moon since he'd been forced to take shelter in the makeshift hut. His wounds were healed and now the weather was melting the snow. Come sunrise, he would leave in his pursuit of the white man and the squaw. There would be no tracks to follow. He would have to rely on his warrior's instinct. North. He would travel north. It was the only thing that made sense.

The morning air was cold. Not freezing, but not much above it. Wrapped in his blankets and wearing snowshoes he'd made, Stares at the Moon headed north with only the revenge in his heart to carry him on.

Because of the snow, the going was slow, but as he saw it, the gods were still smiling on him for they brought game to keep his stomach full and there had been no more storms. Warmer weather was truly on its way. The scalp of the white man would be his and the squaw would feel the power of Stares at the Moon.

During the nights, by the light of his fire, Stares at the Moon was able to make himself a bow and quiver of arrows. The tips were made of stones, and not as good as he would have liked, but they would have to do. He longed for his rifle, but he guessed the white man had taken it. Another thing to get back when he would finally get his revenge

Being in a strange part of the mountains, Stares at the Moon wandered around the forest for six weeks before accidently catching sight of a cabin. He stopped – his breath suddenly coming in gasps. There it stood. It had to be the place he sought. He knew there were other mountain men hereabouts, but his insides told him this was the one he was searching for. The white man and the squaw were inside. They had to be.

Taking a deep breath to calm his nerves, he sat down behind a bush and allowed his body to relax. Now that he'd found them, he could take his time and wait for them to show themselves. Yes, he must plan. There could be no mistakes.

****

Indeed, Lucas and Crying Dove should have been inside the cabin, but with the weather letting up and the snow melting, they had ventured out in search of meat – along with taking in the fresh, high mountain air. They had been couped up inside the cabin for over a month and the fresh, cold air smelled wonderful.

Before leaving, Lucas did as he always did, he left bear traps scattered about - hidden beneath snow, grass, leaves – anything to disguise them. Twice he had come back to find game waiting. And three times he had found evidence of Indians who sought to make a surprise attack.

Stay directly behind me," he told Crying Dove when they left. "Otherwise, you might find your horse snared in a bear trap."

Crying Dove did not need to be told twice. Using a stick, Lucas had shown her what would happen if her horse stepped on one. She had jumped back when the vicious teeth of the trap snapped together, driving the sharp teeth, deep into the stick of wood.

They had left the day before Stares at the Moon happened upon the cabin, so they had no idea he might be close.

One the second day, they were walking a short distance from their camp and spotted a large, male elk with a huge rack. Lucas stopped and stood death-like, still, and Crying Dove did the same. He wasn't sure how long they stood like that, but it seemed, forever. Finally, the elk turned his head away from them just enough to allow Lucas to bring his rifle up to his shoulder and sight in on the elk's left front, shoulder area. He took a deep breath, and as he let it out, he slowly, squeezed the trigger.

The rifle let out a roar and slammed against his shoulder and the elk went down before he had a chance to run away.

Fortunately for Lucas and Crying Dove, the trees were still covered with snow, plus, they were many miles from the cabin, so, Stares at the Moon never heard the gunshot.

Without being told, Crying Dove set about skinning the elk and cutting up the meat while Lucas cut off the antlers. He would have much use for them as knife handles, and other things.

Lucas put the meat in the canvas bags he'd brought with him and made two packs.

The following morning, they loaded the packs on the mule, and headed back down the mountain, happy with their hunting trip. The meat, along with the rolled-up hide, was heavy and more than he wanted to load the mule down with, so he carried the hide on his horse, behind the saddle, while Crying Dove's horse carried the antlers.

The cold weather had not been easy on them and Lucas could tell Crying Dove was feeling the effects from it, but he was proud of the way she made the trip without so much as a whimper. He wished the weather could have been better, but it was what it was. Life in the high elevations could, and usually was, hard on both men and women.

Still one day from the cabin, rain fell as they made their camp for the night. Lucas made a small fire for coffee and they cooked just enough meat to fill their bellies. Using a sheet of canvas he'd brought along for such occasions, he hung it between two trees and made a covering for them to keep the rain off of them, then wrapped themselves in their blankets and slept the sleep of the dead.

Lucas was the first one up. The sky was clear, and he refueled the fire and put coffee on to boil. He lowered the meat from up in the trees where he had stored it so wolves and other meat eaters would not be tempted to try and steal it.

He was slicing off two pieces of meat for their breakfast when Crying Dove came up to him and said, "Let me do this."

Where she found the wild onions and berries, Lucas had no idea, but they went well with the meat and coffee.

Before the sun had cleared the tree tops, Lucas said, "If we leave now, we can be back at the cabin before nightfall – that is if you feel strong enough to ride?"

She smiled at him and said, "Do not worry, white man, I will go where you go and I will not give up until you do."

Lucas felt embarrassed that she thought he was speaking down to her, like Indian men did to their squaws. "I didn't mean it like it sounded," he told her. "I only…"

She put her fingers to his lips and said, "I know. I just want you to know, just because I am a woman, I am not weak."

At that moment, something inside Lucas, stirred. She was quite a woman, this, Crying Dove. Yes, quite a woman indeed.

Fortunately, the path back to the cabin was mostly all, down-hill. Had they been trying to go in the opposite direction, their progress would have been much slower due to the mud and ice. Even so, going downhill was tricky at its best.

****

Stares at the Moon had spent a considerable amount of time, studying the situation. He had seen no movement and wondered if they had died inside the cabin from freezing or lack of food?

Twice, he had considered walking up to the cabin and opening the door, but each time, something held him back. If they weren't dead, he could be walking into a trap – if they had seen him, the white man could be standing on the other side of the door with a gun in his hand and shoot him before he could get away.

Stares at the Moon listened; trying to hear voices inside, but the cabin was as silent as a tomb.

He built himself a small, sheltered, smokeless fire to roast the rabbit he'd killed – and while he was eating, it came to him that he didn't need to try and storm the cabin. He could shoot a fire-arrow onto the roof and set the cabin on fire. In fact, he could shoot several fire-arrows onto the roof. That would drive them out and he could fill their bodies with arrows. Or could he? What if the white man came out with his rifle and began firing at him? His arrows would be no match for the rifle.

The sun was headed for the western tree tops when he heard the voices of a man and a woman.

Stares at the Moon, kicked snow over the fire to put it out, then made himself hidden behind a tree.

Sure enough, as the voices became louder, Lucas and Crying Dove came into view. They looked to be loaded with what appeared to be meat, hide and the antlers of a large elk. But the most astonishing thing to Stares at the Moon, was the fact that the squaw was laughing and talking. She had never done that with him!

Suddenly, Lucas slowed his pace and sniffed the air. Smoke. He smelled smoke. He could see no smoke coming from the chimney of the cabin, so he guessed whoever it was, was still outside – maybe, thinking they were inside. "Do not stop, but we must hurry and get inside the cabin. We have company – possibly the man who stole you from your people," Lucas whispered over his shoulder. "Go in front of me and stay on the path. I will cover us."

Crying Dove needed no encouragement. Just the thought of Stares at the Moon being anywhere near, made her quiver, inside.

As she made her way past him, Lucas held his rifle at the ready, and let his eyes search the nearby trees – but saw nothing or no-one until they were closer to the cabin. There, on the ground was just a whiff of smoke rising into the air.

Without hesitation, Lucas pulled the rifle to his shoulders and snapped off, two quick shots, as he yelled, "Go!"

Stares at the Moon watched in anger as the white man and the squaw rode hell bent for leather to the front of the cabin, and made their way, safely into the cabin. The white man had fired two shots in his direction, but neither shot came close.

Stares at the Moon watched as the three animals ran off into the trees and although he would have liked to have had the meat, he guessed they would run for miles before settling down.

FIVE

Lucas closed and barred the door just as an arrow lodged itself in the outer part with a thud.

"Get behind that wall and hunker down," Lucas shouted at Crying Dove – and without hesitation, she obeyed.

Lucas had his pistol in his hand and peeked through the small openings he'd made for just this sort of thing – but he could see no one.

"Patience," he whispered to himself.

It didn't take long before he saw a small portion of the Indian's head appear from around the far side of a tree – looking directly at the cabin. It was the same Indian he'd fought with – the one who had been beating on Crying Dove.

He waited, hoping for a clear shot at the brave, but he was being very cautious.

"Is it Stares at the Moon?" Crying Dove asked.

"Yes, but don't worry, the cabin is well fortified and if he tries to break in, it will be the biggest mistake he's ever made," Lucas informed her.

Crying Dove slumped back down on the floor. She trusted this white man more than any man she'd ever met – even the braves of her tribe. Except for her father and brothers, he had been kind to her and never tried to force himself on her like every other man she'd known.

"What is he doing?" Crying Dove asked.

"Nothing at the moment," Lucas said, "but I'm guessing he's up to something."

Just then, Lucas saw the smoke rising into the air and said, "I think we have ourselves a problem."

"What do you mean, a problem?" Crying Dove said, standing up and peeking through one of the holes in the wall where a person could shoot through.

"I don't think that fire is to keep him warm," Lucas told her.

Crying Dove got the message, loud and clear. "He means to set the cabin on fire to force us to come out, or stay in here and die, doesn't he?"

"That would be my guess," Lucas said, nodding his head.

Just then, Stares at the Moon stepped out from behind the tree and fired a flaming arrow toward the cabin, then disappeared behind the tree.

The arrow landed on the roof and immediately caught it on fire. The shingles were dry and took no time at all to ignite.

Lucas fired at Stares at the Moon when he launched the second arrow, but he was too late and it landed on another part of the roof, catching it on fire.

Smoke was beginning to fill the cabin as Lucas ran around, filling a pack with things.

"What are we going to do?" she asked.

Lucas had strapped on two rifles and then slung the pack over his shoulders. "Follow me," he said as he ran toward the back of the cabin.

Crying Dove watched as Lucas moved a deerskin hanging on the wall, that reveled a door! One she had never known about.

"My emergency door," he told her. "Come on."

Crying Dove held a piece of rag over her mouth and nose to help her breathing but her eyes were watering so bad it was hard for her to see and she was stumbling around. A piece of the roof landed on her head and she could feel her hair burning. With the rag she had over her mouth and nose, she quickly put out the fire in her hair, then tried to look around, but the cabin was filled with smoke and she became disoriented.

Pieces of wood were falling into the cabin from the flaming roof, setting the interior on fire as Lucas took her by the arm and pressed a bundle into her arms, then gently pulled her along to the back of the cabin.

"Stay close to me," he said as he opened the back door and ushered her through, then followed her, closing the back door. Out of sight from Stares at the Moon, they slipped into the woods.

Crying Dove's eyes were still watering and she was still coughing, but through her squinted eyes, she was able to follow the white man who was becoming more endearing to her with each passing day.

Lucas wasn't in much better shape. His lungs ached and his eyes burned, but he figured it was better than the alternative.

Stares at the Moon studied the front door of the cabin, wondering why they had not tried to escape.

Surely, they would not stay inside and die? Being burned alive was one of the most painful ways to go to the great beyond. Even as the roof caved in on the cabin, the front door stayed closed.

Something wasn't right, but Stares at the Moon couldn't figure out, just what…?

Then it came to him and he felt stupid for not thinking of it, sooner. The white man had a door at the back of the cabin so he could escape if danger came!

He cursed his stupidity as he put out his fire and ran to the backside of the cabin, and saw the door. When he looked toward the forest, he realized the sun had disappeared and there was only a quarter moon.

The forest was dark and there was no way he could track them until morning and the burning cabin was too hot for him to search for their bodies, just in case he had been wrong.

He did, however, take advantage of the heat and made his bedroll as close as he could to the front of the cabin.

SIX

Several, thin strands of light, sneaking through the trees, pressed their way into Stares at the Moon's eyes, bringing him to an abrupt awakness. He sat up and looked around. The cabin was nothing more than a mass of smoldering embers – and still too hot to search.

Standing up, he looked carefully at what used to be the interior of the cabin, his eyes searching for any sign of a body, or skeleton – but he saw only burnt things like chairs and a table.

Stares at the Moon opened his pouch and ate the few berries he had left, then lifted the waterskin to his mouth and drank, deeply. He would need meat, soon, but for now, this would have to do. He was anxious to begin his pursuit of the white man and the squaw.

Just inside the trees, Stares at the Moon found what he was looking for – evidence of two people heading into the forest. He went back and rolled up his bedroll and slung it over his back, then turned and headed for the back of the cabin where he had found evidence of his prey.

He'd taken only a few steps when he heard the snap of the trap and felt the excruciating pain in his left ankle. Again, he cursed his stupidity.

Using all his reserve, Stares at the Moon bent down and opened the jaws of the trap and stepped out of it, then watched as it snapped together, again.

Sitting down on the ground, he inspected his wound and found it bloody, but only bruised. His ankle was not broken. He looked at the sky and thanked the Gods that watched over stupid braves like himself, then set about bandaging his ankle.

On his hands and knees, he crawled around until he found a piece of tree-limb he could use as a crutch. The injury would slow him down, but not stop him from what he meant to do.

Their trail was not difficult to follow. In the dark and their haste to escape, the white man had not bothered to try and cover his tracks. How stupid of him. An Indian would never have made that blunder, he thought as he hobbled along.

Half an hour later, Stares at the Moon came to a halt. Their tracks had disappeared onto a giant mass of bare boulders. After searching both sides of the boulders, he decided they had climbed onto them to make their passage more difficult to follow.

Stares at the Moon looked at the long trail of boulders and wondered how he could cross them in his condition. He hadn't eaten anything except the handful of berries and he was beginning to feel the effects of not having anything of substance in his stomach.

He was making his way over to sit down on one of the boulders when he heard the rattle of a mountain rattlesnake.

Just to his left, he saw the snake, coiled up, it's tail shaking. It was ready to strike. Using the bottom end of his crutch, Stares at the Moon reached out and drove the tip of the crutch against the snake's head, pressing it to the ground, then using his hunting knife, he cut off the head.

It wasn't as big as the rattlesnakes down on the prairie, but it would have to do.

Just inside the tree-line, he found a patch of wild strawberries and after building a fire, he cooked the snake and decided it tasted a lot like prairie chicken.

Between the snake meat and the berries, he felt somewhat revived.

When he finished eating, he drank sparingly from his waterskin – not knowing when he would have a chance to re-fill it, again.

With food in his stomach, Stares at the Moon took a large gulp of air and headed across the huge mass of boulders.

****

Lucas knew this part of the mountains like he knew the area around his cabin and indeed, had come to the large mass of boulders, on purpose. It would be rough going, but he knew a trail in between most of them that would take them up the mountain to higher ground and a place where he could defend them from anyone who pursued them. He dragged a piece of tree limb behind them to wipe out any trace of their passing.

The sun had gone just past its high point when they emerged from the boulders and saw a small ledge jutting out from the side of the mountain.

"Up there," Lucas said, pointing at the ledge. "That's where we're headed."

Crying Dove was exhausted and her breathing labored, but she said nothing – only nodded her head and followed Lucas as he began to climb. There was no path or stairs, although Lucas seemed to know a way. They had to climb almost straight up for a good thirty or forty feet to reach the ledge, and by the time they climbed up over the edge of the ledge, Crying Dove's fingers were bleeding.

Without any complaints, she sat down and looked around. The ledge pushed out from a deep impression into the side of the mountain, like a large room. She could see where Lucas had been here before. There was a firepit, with a stack of wood next to it and in the back, water trickled from a crack in the mountain, into a small pool that didn't overflow, which meant there was a drainage at the bottom of the pool, taking the water to who knew where? And over to one side, she could see what looked like several animal skins rolled up and stacked neatly near the wall. Bedrolls, she wondered?

Along the front edge of the ledge, rocks had been placed to make three, small walls where a person could shoot from, aiming down on an attacker, without leaving themselves open to be shot. Very clever, Crying Dove thought as she stared at the white man she knew as, Lucas. He had brought them here on purpose, knowing Stares at the Moon could not get to them without exposing himself and getting killed.

After carefully looking at their backtrail, Lucas moved over and started a fire in the firepit then looked at Crying Dove.

"If you will, please go through the packs and find the food I've stored there and make us something to eat while I watch the trail for our friend."

"Do you think he is following us?" Crying Dove asked, knowing the boulders they had come through would make it almost impossible to follow them.

"Oh, he'll be coming alright. It just might take him a bit longer than it did us, but he'll be along, shortly," Lucas said with a slight grin. "When he can't find what's left of our bodies in the ashes, he'll be mad at himself for being outfoxed, and want our hides, even more than he did, before."

It was late afternoon when Stares at the Moon smelled the smoke and stopped. Mixed in with the smoke was the smell of meat cooking and his stomach began to grumble. In the mass of boulders, he hadn't seen even one animal to make a meal out of – and the snake he'd eaten that morning had long since stopped giving him nourishment.

He left the boulders and was now in the forest, again, and from where he stood, he could see the open place and the ledge, high up from the ground. Smoke was easing itself out of what looked like a depression and disappearing off into the sky.

Anger welled up inside him as Stares at the Moon realized he'd been outsmarted by the white man, once again. He'd heard stories about these mountain-men knowing the mountains as well as the Indians did, but this was the first one he'd come up against.

He crept close to the edge of the forest so he could get a better look at the ledge. He could see three, short walls blocking any shots he might have – and whoever was behind the walls, would have a clear shot at anyone below.

Stares at the Moon came to realize, the white man had found this place and had made it his place to escape to if there was trouble. He had chosen well for it would be almost impossible to attack.

The sun was making long shadows and Stares at the Moon knew he could do nothing more, this day.

He went back, deeper into the forest where he made himself a small fire, then went into the trees and set three small animal traps made from strips of bark.

He hadn't been sitting next to his fire, long, when he heard the squeal of a rabbit. Smiling, Stares at the Moon went to check on his traps – and in one, he found a good-size rabbit, and in another one, a young, doe. The third trap was empty, but it did not matter. With the doe and the rabbit, he would have enough meat to eat for several days while he tried to figure out how to kill the white man, and take back, the squaw.

SEVEN

Lucas cut off a large piece of meat that was cooking over the fire, and handed it to Crying Dove, who smiled and took it, marveling at this man. Most braves ate first and if there was anything left, the women and children got it. She remembered the nuns at the mission saying that white men treated women different than Indian braves do. And since being rescued by this white man, she was beginning to appreciate the difference.

"He's out there," Lucas said, with juice dripping off his chin. "I heard him, then got a glimpse of him as he stood behind a tree, looking up at the ledge."

Crying Dove was startled to learn this and asked, "Do you think he will wait until he thinks we are asleep, then try and climb up here and kill us?"

Lucas swallowed his piece of meat, then said, "If he does, it will be to kill me, but not you. Oh no, he wants you alive."

When Lucas saw the expression in Crying Dove's eyes, he quickly added, "But I'm not going to let that happen."

"What will you do?" Crying Dove asked. "You cannot stay awake both day and night. You will need to sleep, sometime."

Lucas finished eating his piece of meat, then wiped his fingers on his pantlegs, and grinned. "Don't intend to. That's where you come in. I'm going to lay down over there next to the wall, where it's dark, and go to sleep with my rifle next to me. You're going to sit over against the other wall next to the ledge where you can see if he tries to climb up. If you see any movement down there, any movement at all, you're going to wake me up and I'll do the rest."

Crying Dove had to admit it was a good plan. She was glad he had included her in the plan, and vowed to do a good job. She would be like the hawk and watch for any movement – any sign that Stares at the Moon was trying to sneak up on them.

In just a few moments, she heard snoring coming from the far wall and knew Lucas had gone to sleep.

She, herself, was tired, but could not allow her weariness to overcome her. She had a vital job to do.

Three hours later, Crying Dove was overcome with exhaustion and her eyes closed as she drifted off to sleep.

Something creeped into Lucas' subconscious, telling him to wake up, but his conscious mind said there was nothing to worry about and he fought waking up.

But there was something – a small noise that shouldn't be there.

His eyes opened and he sat up, his pistol in his hand. Then the sound came again and he knew. Crying Dove had fallen asleep and her soft snoring had awakened him.

He was about to go over to her, when he saw a movement, ever so slightly, coming over the edge of the ledge.

He eased up to a standing position and waited and watched from the dark place, with his back against the wall – his pistol, ready – aimed at the man coming over the ledge.

With the slowness of a snail, Stares at the Moon eased himself over the edge of the ledge and lay there, motionless, allowing his eyes to adjust to the dim light given off by the embers of the fire.

The white man was nowhere to be seen, but off to his right, he could see the squaw, leaning against the wall, snoring softly. Where was the white man?

From out of the darkness, Stares at the Moon heard a whispered voice ask, "Looking for me?"

Stares at the Moon lifted himself up and drew the bowstring back on his bow, ready to launch an arrow at the white man, but before he could unleash the arrow, he heard a loud boom and felt pain in his chest as he was knocked backward over the edge of the ledge. He felt no pain as his body careened off the rocks as he fell to the ground below because he was already, dead.

At the sound of the pistol going off, Crying Dove's eyes jerked open and she jumped to her feet in time to see Stares at the Moon go backward, over the edge of the ledge.

She jerked her head in the direction of where Lucas had been sleeping and saw him come walking toward her. She felt shame for falling asleep. She had let her guard down and they could have been killed. She wouldn't blame Lucas if he turned her out for her negligence.

Instead of cursing at her, he looked at her and asked, "Are you alright?"

"I fell asleep. I'm sorry," she said, staring down at her feet.

"It was your snoring that saved us," Lucas said with a chuckle. "Woke me up in time to see him coming over the ledge."

"Still, I should not have been sleeping. I was to stay awake and watch, but I let my tiredness put me to sleep. I should have stayed awake. I will not blame you if you do not want me in your camp, any longer. If you tell me to leave, I will go," Crying Dove told him, her head still bowed, looking at her feet. She was too embarrassed to look at him.

"Nonsense. Could have just as well been me. We were both exhausted," Lucas told her, then said, "We still have several hours before the sun comes up, so, let's get some rest. We'll have plenty to do come sunup."

The sun was up when they heard the yipping of the wolves, fighting over Stares at the Moon's dead body.

Lucas got up and walked over to the edge of the ledge and looked down, then shook his head. From behind him, he heard Crying Dove's voice.

"Is that what I think it is?" she asked.

Lucas gave a sigh. "It is." He lifted his rifle to his shoulder, aimed down at the wolves and shot one of them, scattering the rest.

Within minutes a wolf came back and dragged the dead wolf away.

Lucas looked at Crying Dove and said, "You pack our gear while I go down and cover what's left of him with rocks. I have no shovel here for a proper burial."

Lucas had just finished covering what was left of Stares at the Moon, with rocks when the first pack landed on the ground behind him, followed shortly by the second one – then he watched as Crying Dove climbed down. He was glad she hadn't had to look at what the wolves had done.

"Where do we go, now?" Crying Dove asked.

"Back to the cabin," Lucas said, pointing back down the mountain. "And let's hope the fire didn't spread to the small barn I built off in the trees. And, I'm hoping the horses and the mule headed for there when we turned them lose."

Crying Dove knew he had horses and a mule, but had no idea what he'd done with them when they first came to the cabin. She hadn't remembered him trying to leave the cabin to feed or water them – but she remembered he had brought them to the cabin so they could go on their hunting trip, and she remembered getting off her horse and running into the cabin but had forgotten all about what had happened to them.

She just nodded her head, but said a silent prayer to her God of hope, that they would be there as Lucas wished for.

As they headed into the trees, Crying Dove glanced over her shoulder at the pile of rocks, thinking how things could change in the blink of an eye.

Crying Dove was surprised when they came upon a large structure which was sitting in among the trees. If a person wasn't looking for it, they could have easily walked right on by without ever seeing it.

When they got closer, they heard one of the horses, whinny, and the mule made his breying sound.

"Guess they smelled us coming," Lucas said with a grin.

Inside, the barn was larger than it looked from the outside. There were six stalls along one side of the structure – all standing open. There were stacks of hay on the other wall along with a pipe leading to a water trough where the animals would always have water to drink.

When Lucas saw Crying Dove looking around, he said, "The winters up here can be pretty mean, so I built this place so the animals could spend several months during the winter without me coming out to see to them."

Lucas' horse walked over to him and put his nose against Lucas' chest and snorted.

"Guess you want me to take off my saddle and that load of hide, don't you, ole girl?" Lucas said, patting her neck.

After unpacking, the horses and the mule, Lucas checked the meat. A little of it had turned from being in the canvas packs, but the majority of it was still good, so they would have meat to eat. Unfortunately, they would be in short supply of vegetables – what with the cabin and all its contents, burned to the ground.

While Lucas was spreading out the elk hide so he could clean and cure it, Crying Dove excused herself and left the barn.

Lucas had just spread the elk hide out, and tacked it on the wall to dry, when Crying Dove stepped inside and called out, "Food is ready when you are ready to eat."

Lucas grinned and said, "I'm ready now! I'm hungry enough to eat a horse!" He looked over at the two horses and said, "Just kidding." The mule raised its head and breyed.

Outside, not far from the front of the barn, Crying Dove had built a nice fire and Lucas could see a cast iron pot hanging over the flames.

"What have we, here?" he asked as she handed him a cup of coffee.

"Stew," she told him. "I found a few things in the forest and with the meat, I made a stew. I hope you like it."

She ladled him a bowl full and said, "I'm sorry there is no bread cakes to go with the stew. I know how much you like them. Maybe later when I can find the things I need."

Lucas took a whiff and had to admit, it did smell good – a spicy good, if he wasn't mistaken. He took a spoonful and put it in his mouth, and was instantly, pleased. It had the spiciness he liked and he looked at Crying Dove with a question in his eyes.

"You might be surprised at what you can find in the forest if you know what to look for," Crying Dove informed him as she sat down next to him and began to eat.

Lucas had been up in the mountains for several years and was amazed that he never seemed to stop learning. The mountains and the forest were forever giving him new things to learn. Where she got the spices and other things she put in the stew, he had no idea, but he would make sure she showed him.

A week of sifting through the ashes to find whatever had survived, they came up with precious, little. A skillet and a few pots and pans, plus some handle-less knife blades.

After clearing a spot near the back corner of where the cabin had been, Lucas dug down in the ground and pulled out a leather wrapped box. Inside was all the money he had to his name – almost a thousand dollars, along with a small bag of gold nuggets.

He had yet to find any big strikes of gold in the creeks and nearby rivers, but he had found a little gold, here and there. Fortunately, there was plenty of game and their hides brought a pretty penny. Living up here, there were no places to go spend the money he'd made selling his hides, so he just kept putting it away for the day he would think about going back down to one of the towns to settle down and maybe buy a business of some kind. But each time he went down to Denver, he was reminded of why he loved living in the high elevations where it was quiet and peaceful.

The days passed quickly as they cleared the area where the cabin had been. It was Lucas' plan to rebuild the cabin on the same spot and he began to cut and stack timber for the walls. On a morning when the sun came up bright and warm, Lucas decided it was time to go down to Denver and sell his hides. He would also be taking Crying Dove back to her people, but chose to keep that part, secret, for now.

Crying Dove was amazed at the number of hides Lucas had stored in the barn and as they left, she looked over at him and said, "I have never been to Denver. What is it like? Most of my people say it is a place of wickedness. Some of the men from my tribe went there and became addicted to the white man's fire water. Are you addicted to it?"

Lucas glanced over his shoulder and said, "I like a drink from time to time, but, no, I am not addicted to liquor. And as far as what Denver is like, I have to agree with your people, it can be a wicked city if you let it to get to you. As far as what it's like – well, it's different than an Indian camp in many ways. In an Indian camp, there are no stores, or dancehalls, or churches and such, like there are in a big city, like Denver and other cities around the country. Plus, there are more people than you can count. Some good and some bad. I think, in many ways, an Indian camp is a much better place to live. Although, I prefer living up in the mountains where there is quiet and solitude."

Crying Dove took it all in and let it filter through her brain, coming to the conclusion that she too, would prefer living up on the mountain away from all the sin and wickedness she'd heard about - as long as Lucas was there, too. On some days, she missed her mother and father along with some of her friends, but in the end, she felt safe and content waking each morning to Lucas' smiling face.

That night, as he sat around the campfire, sipping coffee, after their meal - Lucas watched as Crying Dove cleaned up and knew he would miss her. Not only was she a good cook, she had become dear to him in more ways than one. He also knew she would gladly stay with him, but it wasn't right. She needed to be with her people, or at least, be allowed to have the opportunity to do so.

Denver proved to be just what Lucas thought it would be – noisy and filled with people from all walks of life. There were other mountain men there, selling their hides and other things they'd made, such as knives of several sizes. A few of them had gold to trade for money or goods. The dancehalls were filled to capacity with men readily parting with their hard-earned money, or gold, not caring that they would be broke by the time they went back into the mountains or ranches where they worked.

Because of the way Lucas tanned his hides, he got top dollar for them and went to the mercantile store and purchased what he would need to take back up to the high country, including a new saw, hammer, nails and other things he would need to rebuild his cabin. He even went so far as to buy a wagon to haul the things he'd bought, like a cast iron stove, a table and four chairs, new kerosene lamps, cooking utensils, and such.

Crying Dove was astounded by the number of things Lucas purchased, thinking they would be living in luxury.

"Life will be so much easier now," she told him over supper at a restaurant not far from the hotel, where she got stares from the white people eating there. He'd even had to have a heart-to-heart talk with the owner of the hotel so he would allow an Indian to stay there.

Having lived among the Indians on several occasions, Lucas knew them to be basically, just like

67

anyone else – not the savages the white people claimed them to be. So, when he went out of his way to make sure Crying Dove was treated fairly - he'd gone so far as to dress her in white people's clothes.

It was a cool night and they were taking their time, strolling along the sidewalk on their way to the hotel, allowing Crying Dove to look in the store windows and marvel at all of the things there was to buy.

They were standing in front of a women's dress shop when a cowboy came out of a nearby saloon and headed in their direction. When he got close, he stopped and stared at Crying Dove. Lucas was standing at the shop window next to the dress shop, looking at new saddles, so the drunken cowboy didn't associate Lucas with the Indian squaw.

The cowboy reached up and stroked Crying Dove's hair, saying, "Hey, pretty little papoose, how about you come up to my room and we can have ourselves a time?"

Crying Dove whirled around and pushed the cowboy's hand away. "I am not that kind of woman."

The cowboy grabbed her by the wrist and said, "You're an Indian and Indian squaws ain't allowed ta say, no. Now come with me or I'll have to rough you up some to make you see yer duty."

"No! Let go of me!" Crying Dove shouted, which got Lucas' attention.

Lucas ran over and pulled the cowboy's hand loose and said, "Leave her be. She's with me!"

The cowboy looked at Lucas and said, "No. You ain't cutting in. I was here first. Go find yer own squaw. This'uns goin' with me," and went for his pistol.

Before the cowboy could clear his pistol from the holster, he found Lucas' fist driving against his jaw, sending him sprawling into the street where he landed on his back.

Enraged, Lucas followed the cowboy and when he pulled his pistol, Lucas kicked the gun from his hand.

The cowboy rolled over and came to his feet. "Anything I like better'n whiskey or a woman, is a good fight. So, let's have at it."

Lucas took stock of the man he was about to bust knuckles with and realized he was at least six feet tall and probably weighed close to two hundred pounds.

With his fist in a fighting position, the cowboy circled around Lucas, looking for an opening to Lucas' jaw.

Lucas feigned a jab with his left, then drove a right into the cowboy's stomach, thinking to knock the wind out of him, but it was like hitting a rock wall.

The cowboy laughed and smashed his fist against the side of Lucas' head, knocking him sideways.

Pain radiated throughout Lucas' head and he almost went down. It felt more like being kicked by a mule than hit with a fist.

Lucas looked up just in time to see the cowboy coming at him to finish him off, and just in the nick of time, Lucas ducked under another of those huge fists.

Lucas circled around, trying to get his eyes to focus correctly and when he did, he realized he could not fight this man in a normal toe to toe slugfest.

In his peripheral vision, he saw Crying Dove standing on the sidewalk, fear in her eyes. They had also attracted a good-size crowd of town folks walking down the street.

The cowboy was coming at him, again, and this time, Lucas ducked under the swing and came around to the back of him, then leaped onto his back and stuck his thumbs in the man's eyes and pressed hard.

The cowboy let out a loud scream, then grabbed Lucas by the hair on his head and jerked him over his shoulder, slinging him to the ground.

Lucas leaped to his feet and saw the man rubbing his eyes – and took advantage of the situation by driving the knuckles of his fingers into the man's throat.

Now the cowboy couldn't see or breathe, which allowed Lucas to throw all his weight into the punch to the man's jaw.

The big cowboy staggered back a few paces, then toppled over on his back, out like the light in his brain had been turned off.

Without a word, Lucas walked up on the sidewalk, took Crying Dove by the arm and walked off toward the hotel. People's whispers filled the air. The fight would be the subject of conversation for some time to come. Although, Crying Dove would never mention it, deep in her heart, she felt pride in the fact that Lucas would fight for her.

Come morning, after breakfast, Lucas checked out of the hotel, saddled their two horses and told Crying Dove to get on her horse.

The fact that Lucas had done nothing about the wagon filled with furniture and such, caused Crying Dove to become, curious. "Where are we going?" she asked as they rode down the street.

"You'll see," Lucas told her, still not wanting to tell her he was taking her back to her people.

Crying Dove did as she was told and rode along in silence, but her mind was working overtime, wondering what Lucas was up to?

Late that afternoon, many miles south of Denver they topped over a rise and Crying Dove pulled her mount to a halt and stared.

At the bottom of the hill, she could see the people of her village, moving about as fear welled up inside her. "No!" she said. "I do not want to go back to my people."

"Why?" Lucas asked. "I thought you'd be happy to get back to them."

Crying Dove looked at Lucas with tears rolling down her cheeks. "I am happy being with you, but I must confess, I have dreamed many times about being back with my people and my friends, but it never can be."

"Why?" Lucas asked, again.

Crying Dove gave a sigh, then said, "Because, in my people's eyes, I am a disgraced woman."

"What? That's ridiculous," Lucas said. "They're your people."

"When I was captured by the Sioux brave, Stares at the Moon, the Arapahoe knew my fate and I could no longer be a woman of the Arapahoe tribe. To them I am disgraced. And now, I am with you – a white man. They will never accept me."

Lucas was about to speak when out of the trees, six Arapahoe braves rode out with rifles pointed at them.

One of them spoke to Crying Dove and pointed his rifle in the direction of the camp.

When they rode into the camp, people stared at them and followed along to the chief's teepee.

The chief, a tall, rawboned man in his forties, came out and stared at them for some time before looking over at a man and woman standing nearby.

Crying Dove followed the chief's look and saw her mother and father standing there. Her father had a scowl on his face and her mother was crying. She looked up at Crying Dove with a look that said she wanted to take Crying Dove in her arms and hold her, but knew she could not do so.

"Why have you returned?" Chief, Dark Wolf, asked in the Arapahoe tongue, pointing his finger at her.

Crying Dove looked at him and realized it was just as she had predicted. To them, she was dead. "This white man rescued me from the Sioux brave and he brought me back, thinking you would welcome me."

"You are disgraced - and to us you are dead," Dark Wolf stated matter of factly.

What the chief, or even, Crying Dove, didn't know that over the years, Lucas had learned to speak several of the Indian languages and Arapahoe was one of them and he had listened to the conversation, knowing he had made a mistake bringing her back.

He reached out to take the rein of Crying Dove's horse in his hand so he could lead it away, but before he could, two braves grabbed him and dragged him off his horse.

Lucas fought like a wounded bear, but in the end, he was no match for the large group of braves who swarmed down on him like locust on a cornfield.

He was dragged over and tied to a pole, then one of them grabbed him by the hair on his head and scalped a place a good three inches across, from the top of his head.

He held it up and danced around, singing a chant as blood seeped from the wound and ran down Lucas' face.

Crying Dove had also been pulled from her horse and was being pushed and shoved by the women of the tribe. Some were hitting her with sticks. Crying Dove tried to fight back, but like Lucas, she was overpowered by numbers.

When night came, and the camp got quiet, Lucas was repeatedly shaking his head, trying to rid it of the flies attacking the bloody spot on the top where he'd been scalped.

He too, had been beaten and jabbed with sharp sticks, creating wounds and welts on his body. He was hungry, thirsty and sore. Since being tied to the stake, he had been, repeatedly, trying to work his hands back and forth, hoping to loosen his bonds enough to get his hands, free. He had tried so hard that he could feel the blood seeping down onto his hands, which he figured could be a good thing. If they got wet enough, the hide he was tied with, might stretch enough to get his hands, free – but that was not to be.

Days turned into weeks – weeks turned into months.

Lucas was treated like a slave and made to do all the dirty work neither the men or the women wanted to do. He was beaten on a constant basis and fed only enough to keep him alive, enough to do their bidding. Even such a menial job as collecting firewood, would bring him pain and embarrassment, because the women would follow him and slap him with switches made from tree limbs and tell him to work faster.

Braves would come by when he was doing women's work, like grinding grain for flour, and curse him, and call him, squaw-woman. Children would throw rocks at him.

Normally, Lucas had no animosities against the Indians, but he came to hate the people of this tribe.

Winter came and when he hung limply from the post he was tied to, nearly frozen, Lucas was moved inside a teepee where there was at least a fire to keep him from freezing. Several times he almost wished they would have let him freeze, but then his hatred would kick in and he waited for the day he could escape and bring down his wrath on them.

The most embarrassing thing for Lucas was the fact that they had stripped him naked and the women would come by and giggle while poking him with sticks.

When spring finally arrived, Lucas was moved back outside and once again, tied to the pole. By now, he was not much more than skin and bones that was covered with welts.

During all this time, Crying Dove was also treated as a slave, but not to the extinct Lucas was. Her heart ached each day as she watched Lucas' strength evaporate little by little from the lack of food and the hard work and beatings he took. By the time they moved him back outside, she had decided to plead with the chief to set him free.

"He's paid for what he did," she told Dark Wolf when she was serving him food.

He laughed and said, "The white man will not have paid for what he did until I see his body lying on the ground with no more life left in it – along with you beside him. Now go, before I decide to end your miserable life this very day…"

On that day, Crying Dove made a promise to herself that she would find a way to free him, even if it meant her own life.

Nearly a week had gone by when her opportunity came.

The moon was high in the sky: millions of stars twinkled overhead when Crying Dove sneaked away from her sleeping hides and belly-crawled a safe distance away from the teepee she shared with three other captives – all white women.

She would have liked to help them escape, too, but she wasn't entirely sure she would be successful with helping Lucas, escape.

Crying Dove made her way as silently as she could up to the backside of the pole where Lucas was tied, and waited until the brave guarding Lucas, turned away.

Lucas heard Crying Dove's whisper. "Do not move. I am here to cut you free."

Lucas felt her cut the rawhide that bound his wrist together… and he felt an exhilaration that made him want to shout - but still, he did not move nor make any sounds, for the brave standing nearby would hear him and call for help. Besides, he wasn't sure what Crying Dove had in mind.

"There is a horse tied in the trees behind you. When I distract the guard, run to the horse and make your getaway," she whispered.

"No," Lucas whispered. "I will not leave without you."

"We cannot both escape," Crying Dove whispered.

"Then we will both die," Lucas hissed. "I will not leave you here!"

There was a long silence, as Crying Dove felt the happiness inside her. He would rather die than leave without her.

Crying Dove whispered, "As you wish. I will go with you, but we must somehow distract the guard."

Lucas thought for a moment, then whispered, "Put your knife in my hand."

When she'd done as he'd asked, Lucas whispered, "Now, slip back away and go to the horse and wait."

Again, Crying Dove did as he asked, but whispered, "Be careful, Snake in the Grass is a powerful warrior and he will not hesitate to kill you."

Lucas counted to twenty-five and when he guessed she was no longer able to be seen, he raised his head and said, "Water. I need water."

Snake in the Grass walked over to Lucas, carrying a waterskin and held it out to Lucas. "Is this what you ask for?" he said in English.

"Yes. Please, my throat is very dry," Lucas told him.

The brave shook his head and said, "First, I must test it to make sure it is good for you to drink."

He lifted the skin to his mouth and took a healthy drink, then lowered the skin and said, "I do not think this is good for white men." He then leaned his head back and began to laugh.

His laughter was choked off by the blade of Crying Dove's knife slicing across his throat. His eyes went wide and he dropped the waterskin, then dropped to the ground, blood staining the area around his neck.

Lucas turned and was just starting toward where Crying Dove would be waiting for him when a brave came out of his teepee to relieve himself and in the moonlight, saw Lucas heading for the trees.

"At-say!" he yelled, which meant, stop. When Lucas continued running, the young brave ran inside his teepee and grabbed his rifle – all the while, yelling to wake up the others.

In the moonlight, Lucas saw Crying Dove sitting on the horse and ran over and tried to leap up behind her, but he was too weak, and fell to the ground. "Go!" he yelled, looking up at her as a rifle shot sounded in the air.

Instead of racing off to save her own life, Crying Dove jumped down and helped Lucas to his feet, then boosted him up onto the horses back, then climbed up behind him, as bullets cut through the trees all around them.

Their lives were spared only because the young brave was a lousy shot and between his excitement and the darkness in the trees, all his shots went wide.

Once Crying Dove was up behind him, Lucas slapped his feet against the big horse's side and felt him leap into a dead run, already, excited by the sound of the rifle shots, which now were several as other braves had come out and were now shooting at them, too. Fate, or the fact that most Indians were poor shots, was what allowed them to get away without being wounded, or killed.

Once they were a short distance away from the Arapahoe camp, Lucas turned the horse in a more northerly direction and headed toward Denver.

The horse had gone less than a quarter of a mile when the roar of a rifle being fired filled the air and Crying Dove was driven against Lucas' back.

"Keep going!" she yelled as she wrapped her arms around his waist and held on as best as she could.

What she didn't know was that the bullet had entered her left side and had gone all the way through her body and lodged itself in Lucas' back – not far from his spine.

He knew he'd also been hit, but now was not the time to stop – not with the angry braves practically breathing down their necks.

After about a mile, Crying Dove felt Lucas lean forward and throw his arms around the horse's neck, trying not to fall off.

"What's wrong?" Crying Dove asked, feeling weak, herself.

"Somehow, I too have been shot," he said, over his shoulder.

Lucas was feeling weakened from the loss of blood, but he was still strong enough to grab the reins and guide the horse to a ditch and down into it. It was a good size ravine and deep enough so they would not be seen in the moonlight.

After a short distance, he pulled the horse to a stop and got down, then helped Crying Dove down.

Sure enough, he could feel the bullet lodged in his back. And luckily, it was just a little under the skin, but bleeding freely.

Lucas looked around and found a stick and held it up to his mouth, saying, "I will put this stick in my mouth and bite down on it, while you get that piece of lead out of my back."

Lucas put the stick between his teeth and bit down, then felt the tip of the knife being pushed into his back and twisted. It was all he could do to keep from passing out. He clamped down on the stick, so hard, he felt it snap in two.

"I got it," Crying Dove said as she held up the bullet for him to see. "You were very brave. Now we need to bandage our wounds and then get far away from here before they find us."

Lucas spit out the broken stick and said, "You are right. If we don't patch up the holes in our bodies, we will probably bleed to death which would give them a great satisfaction."

Crying Dove reached down and tore off a bottom piece of the dress she was wearing and bandaged Lucas' wound, then tore off another piece and handed it to Lucas, who plugged the two holes, then wrapped the rest of the cloth around her waist.

By the time they finished, they were both breathing hard. They'd lost a lot of blood and their strength was waning.

"We've lost a lot of blood and we need meat to rebuild our strength," Lucas said, sitting down on the side of the bank. "Plus, I need some clothes," he said, looking down at his nakedness.

Crying Dove was also feeling very weak, but was able to move over to the horse and remove two sacks hanging over the horse's front shoulders and sat them down next to Lucas.

Lucas was surprised. In all the commotion and it being dark out, he hadn't noticed the bags.

"What's this?" he asked as Crying Dove was opening the sacks and removing the contents.

She smiled and removed a pair of pants and a shirt from one of the bags and handed them to Lucas. "Here, I hope they fit. They belonged to a hostage who will no longer need them.

Because of his weight loss, the pants were big around the waist and several inches too long in the legs, but they were better than running around, naked. She handed him a piece of rope to use as a belt. The shirt had what appeared to be a bullet hole in the back and there were blood stains around the hole.

"Looks like we know what happened to him," Lucas said, pulling on the shirt.

"I'm sorry, but I couldn't find any shoes or boots, or a hat for you," she told him.

"Quiet!" Lucas whispered… as he got up and went to the horse and put his hand over the horse's nose to keep it from whinnying.

Crying Dove listened and then she heard it too – the sound of running horses.

The sound got louder and louder until it passed by, no more than twenty or so feet from the ravine.

When the sound of running horses disappeared into the night, Lucas took his hand away from the horse's nose and said, "That was close."

Crying dove beckoned Lucas over to where she was and handed him a piece of cooked meat and a small, round piece of bread. "Maybe this will help us get our strength back," she told him.

Lucas looked at Crying Dove and said, "You are an amazing woman, Crying Dove."

She was lucky it was dark or Lucas would have seen her blush.

"It is just a few things I thought you might need. And now it will have to do for both of us."

Just then, a thought came to her and she said, "Oh, I almost forgot."

She reached in one of the bags and pulled out a pistol and handed it to Lucas. "I do not know if it works, but I brought it along, just in case it would be helpful to you."

Lucas took the pistol and stared at it. It was nothing like the cap and ball, black powder pistols he was used to shooting. This one was smaller, with a cylinder that held six small bullets.

"You say you found this with the clothes?" Lucas asked.

Crying Dove nodded her head and said, "Yes. It was with the pants and shirt."

Lucas turned it over in his hand, then raised it and sighted down the barrel. "The man who owned this must have come out from back east, somewhere, because this has to be one of the newer models you can only get back there."

"Can you use it?" Crying Dove asked.

Lucas pointed it at an invisible target and said, "The bullets are smaller than what I'm used to, but, hitting a man in the right spot, yes, I do believe it would kill him. So, to answer your question – yes, at least for six shots, unless you happened to find more ammunition for the pistol?"

Crying Dove shook her head. "I'm sorry. That was all there was."

"Well then, it will have to do, and if we get into a skirmish, hopefully I can collect a pistol or rifle with ammunition."

The food and water helped them feel better. Not that they were at full strength, but they were strong enough to travel at a slow pace.

"Feel like traveling?" he asked.

Crying Dove took a moment, then said, "I will be ready when you are."

Lucas looked at the sky and saw they still had several hours of darkness and said, "I think we need to find a place to hide before the sun comes up. Traveling out here on the plains during daylight hours is not in our favor. We can be spotted too easily. It will be better if we can hide during the day and travel at night where we are less likely to be seen."

EIGHT

Shortly before the sun made its appearance on the eastern horizon, they found a small stand of trees. It was a mixture of Elm and Weeping Willow trees, which made it a good place to hide.

Because of the Weeping Willows, they were afforded invisibility from even a short distance.

"We'll spend the day, there," Lucas said, pointing at the small stand of trees.

Once they were inside the trees, they were astounded to find a small, underground fed pond, filled with good drinking water.

Lucas looked up at the sky and said, "Thank you."

Crying Dove made a small, smokeless fire and put the meat they had left, on to warm up, then went looking around.

Using the front part of her dress like an apron, she returned with it filled with wild onions, strawberries, asparagus, mushrooms, some nuts and several Buffalo gourds.

Using her knife, she made cups and a bowl out of the gourds, then commenced to make a stew out of the things she'd found, along with cutting up the meat and adding it to the stew.

And when they finished eating, using the nuts for dessert, she heated water in the gourd bowl, and washed and re-bound Lucas' wound – then he did the same for her, and took special notice that the wounds were not showing any signs of being infected.

"I think we're going to make it," he told her with a grin.

Crying Dove smiled and said, "If the gods are willing… Yes."

Lucas peeked out through the foliage and looked across the vast prairie to make sure he could see no enemy, then turned back and said, "We'd best try and get some sleep. We'll leave as soon as it gets dark."

Crying Dove, feeling safe, fell instantly asleep and slept like a contented child, while Lucas dosed, off and on, constantly listening for the sound of horses.

Twice, he'd gotten up to find out what the noises were that woke him up. The first was a small herd of deer that came to the pond to drink, but turned and ran away when they smelled the fire.

Lucas thought about shooting one of them so they would have meat, but changed his mind. The sound would attract anyone nearby, which they didn't want – especially if it happened to be the Arapahoe braves – plus, it would use one of their precious bullets.

The second time, it was a small herd of Buffalo – maybe three or four hundred. They even woke up Crying Dove, who said, "It would be nice if we had Buffalo meat to eat, but even a small one would be more meat than we could carry – plus it would take us several days to cook it, and we have only one horse to carry us, along with the meat and hide, which it could not do."

Lucas had been giving that a lot of thought. The horse she'd chosen was small, compared to the horses used by the plain's cowboys. And even though they had both lost a lot of weight, their combined weight was over two hundred pounds – which was all right as long as they went slow and for short distances. But, if they were being chased, the poor beast would falter after a short, hard run.

By now it was too late in the afternoon to think about going back to sleep, so they packed up what little they had and drank their fill of water. Lucas' idea was to travel north in the direction of Denver and hope that, along the way, they could find white people who might help them.

The moon was just beyond the horizon when they rode out, cautiously. The horse seemed well rested and eager to go – but Lucas held it to an easy lope.

As they rode along, Lucas let his mind wonder. What would they do if they came upon a ranch, or a town? They had no money to pay for anything. That had all been lost. And he had no more hides or money up at his place, high up in the Rockies, if they could by some stretch of the imagination, get there. He knew there was a strong chance the Indians would find them, first, which, after a short fight, would be their demise.

Just before daylight, they topped a small rise and saw the brightness of a campfire in the distance.

Crying Dove looked at Lucas and said, "It is the braves from my village. They still seek us."

Lucas looked at the sky and knew it would be daylight within the hour and as far as he could see, there was no place for them to hide.

He turned the horse back down the way they came from and at the bottom of the hill, he headed east at a ground eating lope for a good half a mile. By the time he slowed down, the horse was gasping for air and feeling the effects of the run. Still, there was no place for them to hide.

Lucas noticed the wild prairie grass here, was close to three or more feet high. "We'll hide here," he told Crying Dove.

"Where?" she asked. "I see no place to hide."

Lucas got down and helped Crying Dove down, then forced the horse to lay down, then motioned for Crying Dove to lay down next to the horse. And with that done, Lucas lay down close to the horse's head so he could cover its nostrils if need be.

From a distance, all a person would see is the waving of the prairie grass swaying with the wind.

In less than an hour, they heard the sound of horses running in the distance – and moving away from them.

Lucas waited for a good half an hour before he stood up and looked around. In the far distance to the south of them, he saw the tell-tale rise of dust as the Arapahoe braves rode in that direction.

"Come," he told Crying Dove, "Since they are going south, we can now travel by day in the hopes of finding a town or ranch."

While Lucas' plan was sound, he'd forgotten about one thing – the Sioux.

Just before the sun was directly overhead, Lucas and Crying Dove were heading into the lower hills that eventually would turn into mountains. They were riding at a slow pace so as to not wear the horse down, too quickly.

At the bottom of one of the hills there was a small valley with a stream running through it and they headed for it.

But at the same time, a small band of Sioux braves on a hunting trip, came into the valley and headed to the same stream.

Lucas saw them and turned the horse back, but he was too late, they had seen him, too.

He stopped the horse and dismounted with the pistol in his hand, ready to defend them, then counted eleven braves. He had six bullets. The odds were not in his favor.

They stopped twenty feet or so in front of him and looked down the barrel of the pistol in the white man's hand.

The leader of the group, Running Elk, looked at the skinny, ragged looking white man, then over at the young-looking squaw still sitting on her horse and wondered how they came to be together?

"Do you speak Sioux?" Running Elk asked.

"Some," Lucas replied.

"Then you know you are outnumbered and your puny little handgun can only shoot one of us before we kill you, white man."

Lucas smiled and said, "That's where you're wrong. This here pistol shoots six bullets as fast as I can pull the trigger – which means, you might kill me, but you and five of your followers will die today. So, the question is, who of your followers are prepared to die with you, today?"

And since Lucas had spoken in the Sioux language, all of them heard and understood his words.

Running Elk thought for a long time and was not pleased with the way things were going. "What if we trade with you. Your life for the squaw?"

Without thinking about it, Lucas said, "No. The woman belongs to me and I will not trade her. But here's what I will do. You go one way and we'll go another and no one has to die, today."

Running Elk could see the wisdom in what the white man said, but his pride wouldn't let him ride away feeling defeated. The squaw was young and very pleasant on the eyes and he wanted her. "I am not afraid to die, white man," he said with a snarl.

He said this to impress the young woman, and when he saw no response, he felt the anger rising inside him. He would show her who the mightier warrior was. "I say we fight in single combat – knives - just you and me, our wrists tied together by a sort piece of rope so we cannot be far apart. What say you, white man? Will you fight me, Indian style, or hide behind your firearm like a coward?"

Crying Dove got a lump in her throat. She wanted to call out to Lucas to say, no, but knew she could not. Men had their pride and even wounded and his strength less than normal from his loss of blood, she knew what his answer would be. She was both proud and sad at the same time. Proud that he would fight to keep her, yet sad that because of his wound, he would more than likely lose, costing him his life. She sat, silently on her horse, knowing if Lucas lost, she would kick her horse in the sides and try to escape.

Lucas glanced over in Crying Dove's direction and saw the worry in her eyes. Giving her to this Indian brave would be no different than it was when she was with Staring at the Moon.

He wasn't afraid to fight this brave, but what concerned him was his wound. It hadn't had time to heal and the excursion of fighting would just aggravate it and cause it to start bleeding again. Plus, he knew he hadn't regained his strength, yet. He would need to make sure he ended it quickly.

There it was. He'd made his decision. He was about to speak when Running Elk spoke up. "Have you lost your tongue, or is it your courage you have lost?"

Lucas looked up at him and said, "No. I have not lost my tongue. I was just thinking what an unfair fight it will be, since I am very skilled at that kind of fighting. Maybe you should think of something different – something that will give you a fighting chance."

Lucas watched as the Indian brave's eyes squinted in thought.

He was doing exactly what Lucas hoped for – wondering if the white man was as skilled at knife fighting as he claimed.

Running Elk looked at the braves behind him and saw they were watching to see what he would do?

He had named the fight and he couldn't back down, now, without losing face. Filling his voice with as much confidence as he could muster, he said, "We will fight as I said and see who the better warrior is."

He then slid down from his horse and cut one of the reins to use to tie them together.

One of the other braves tied them together, then stepped back and raised his hand.

Both men crouched, ready for the fight to begin, and waited.

When the brave dropped his hand, Running Elk jerked on the rope, yanking the white man toward him and at the same time, thrusting his knife at the man's stomach. It was an old trick that worked against inexperienced fighters, but Lucas was not an inexperienced fighter. He had, indeed fought knife fights with several braves, tied together with short pieces of rope, and had never lost a fight, and didn't plan on losing this one.

Expecting the jerk, Lucas spun around to the backside of Running Elk and instead of being stuck in the stomach, he drove his knife into the brave's side, puncturing his liver.

Running Elk's eyes went wide as he tried to turn to face the white man, but he was jerked backward and fell onto the ground, singing his death song, which lasted only a short time before he gave a sigh and died.

Lucas gave a silent thank you to the man upstairs for allowing him to end this fight, quickly, before he, himself, got hurt or opened his wound.

Lucas untied the rope that bound them together and walked over to where Crying Dove still sat on the horse. He smiled up at her, then turned to the Indians still sitting on their ponies, stunned by what had happened, and said, "Take your friend back to your camp and tell your people he died like a brave man – a warrior. Sing his praises for his bravery, for did I not tell him of my skill? Yet he chose to fight me, anyway."

None of the braves spoke a word. They slid off their horses and put Running Elk across his horse, belly down, then tied his hands to his feet with a rope running under the horse's stomach so he wouldn't fall off during the journey.

Lucas and Crying Dove watched as they rode away and when they were no longer in sight, Crying Dove slid off the horse and ran to Lucas, hugging him. "I was so scared," she said, pushing her face against his chest.

Reluctantly, Lucas allowed himself to put his arms around her, and hold her close to him.

"I really shouldn't be doing this," he said to himself, but he couldn't seem to stop.

They stood that way for what seemed to be a long time – then Crying Dove stepped back and asked, "What of your wound?"

And before Lucas had time to answer, she pulled his shirt up and began inspecting the bandage for blood seepage, but found none.

"It is good. You ended the fight quickly and did not re-open your wound. You are a skilled fighter, Lucas Penny."

Lucas turned her around and looked into her eyes, and saw the same thing he was feeling. He reached out and lifted her face upward, then leaned down and kissed her.

She had never been kissed on the mouth before and the feeling that went through her was nothing like she'd ever experienced before. It was exhilarating and she threw her arms around his neck and kissed him back.

They mounted the horse and rode northward as the sun began to hunt for the western horizon.

Shortly, by the light of the moon, they found a small creek and decided to spend the night.

When morning came, Crying Dove did not want to get up. She wanted to stay, snuggled close to Lucas. It had been a glorious night and she didn't want it to end, and pretended to still be asleep when Lucas shook her, lightly. "Time to be on the go," he told her as he reached down and kissed her on the ear.

NINE

Hollister Evans was standing at the corral fence, watching as one of his men was trying to break a two-year-old mare, who was having none of it. She had thrown the man twice and was in the process of doing it, again.

Movement caught Hollister's peripheral vision and he turned his head to see a dirty, white man, who looked much the worse for wear, sitting astride an Indian pony. His clothes were too big for him and he had on no shoes or boots. Behind him, with her arms around the man's waist, sat a young, Indian squaw.

He watched as they rode up close to him and stopped. Hollister spit a stream of tobacco juice into the dust, then said, "You look like you've had a time of it, Mister."

Lucas took a deep breath, knowing exactly what he looked like. He looked down at the rancher, a man of maybe fifty – six feet tall, and a little over weight, but still a force to be reckoned with. "I have. And I could use your help."

Hollister Evans had been the son of a Baptist, hell-fire and brimstone preacher from Columbus, Ohio, and had run off at the age of fourteen. He'd worked as a drover, a cowboy, and finally, a mountain man until he had enough money to buy a piece of land and build a life for himself. Over the last twenty years, Hollister Evans had worked hard, fought Indians and cattle rustlers, alike, to get the ranch in shape. He'd seen a good many things during that time, but here was a new mystery.

Hollister spit another stream of tobacco juice in the dirt, then said, "Climb down and bring the woman with you. We'll go up to the kitchen and I'll have the cook put some grub together for you while you tell me all about it."

Crying Dove was reluctant to get down, but with Lucas' encouragement, she slid off the horse and followed him.

Lucas couldn't believe their luck. Most white men wouldn't have let an Indian squaw onto their property, let alone, take them in and feed them.

When they followed Hollister into the kitchen, Lucas stopped and stared. The cook was a Chinaman! He was small, with a pig-tail that hung down to his waist.

Chin How, took one look at Lucas and Crying Dove and put his fingers to his nose.

"Whee, dey stink. Chin How no feed until they cleaned up. Dey stink up my kitchen!" And with that, he folded his arms across his chest to prove his point.

Hollister turned and looked at Lucas and Crying Dove, and said, "He does have a point. Follow me."

Out, next to the bunkhouse there was a very large drum sitting up on a platform, that had a spigot facing down into a small area made from planking.

"I had the boys fix this up so they could take a shower when they come in from the range," Hollister said, proudly. There's soap and towels inside the shower area. Do you have clean clothes to change into?"

Lucas looked down at the ground, embarrassed, and said, "No-sir. All we've got is what is on our backs."

Hollister sized them up and looked at Crying Dove, saying, "My wife passed on a few years back, but my daughter, Leslie, is about your size and I'm sure she can find something for you if you're willing to wear a white woman's clothes."

In her best English, Crying Dove smiled and said, "That is very kind of you. I'm so sorry about your wife's passing, and I would be honored to wear your daughter's clothes."

"Ho, ho," Hollister said. "You speak good English! That's good. Yes, very good indeed."

He then looked at Lucas and yelled, "Henry!"

In the blink of an eye a cowboy about Lucas' size came out of the bunkhouse and said, "Yes, boss?"

Hollister looked at him and said, "This man is in bad need of some clean clothes and a pair of boots. Think we can rustle up some duds for him?"

The man called, Henry, sized up Lucas and said, "Yes-sir. I do believe we can," then turned and went back inside the bunkhouse, calling over his shoulder. "I'll be out with them by the time you've finished cleaning up."

Hollister looked at Crying Dove and said, "You come with me."

She looked at Lucas, who nodded his head, yes, then followed the man into the house.

Hollister's daughter had taken an instant liking to her and after Crying Dove showered, Leslie noticed the wound and cleaned and put on a fresh dressing on it. The dress she selected was light-blue and fit Crying Dove like it had been made for her. Leslie combed Crying Dove's hair until it glistened and fell down across her shoulders, making her brown eyes shine.

Crying Dove had also liked this young white woman, who was about her own age and she told her the whole story of what had happened to them. "And that is how we came to ride into your yard," Crying Dove said, looking at herself in the full-length, mirror, liking what she saw.

"You poor, dear!" Leslie exclaimed. She then laughed and said, "Come, let's get you down to the kitchen, you must be starving!"

When she entered the kitchen, her eyes went immediately to Lucas, who was sitting at the table, having a cup of coffee, and her heart soared. He looked so handsome.

Lucas almost spit out the coffee in his mouth. Crying Dove was at that moment, the most beautiful woman he'd ever laid his eyes on.

He jumped to his feet and said, "My Gawd-a-mighty! You look beautiful! No! Even more than that, if it can be!"

Before any more pleasantries could be spoken, Chin How said, "Sit down. Eat before food gets cold. Chin How no serve cold food unless fixed that way!"

Hollister drank coffee and waited while they ate. He chuckled to himself as he watched them clean their plates to the point where they almost didn't need to be washed.

After eating, Leslie took Crying Dove off to do whatever young women on a ranch, do.

As Hollister took Lucas into his office, he asked, "You a drinking man?"

Lucas grinned and said, "Does a hungry man like a good steak?"

Hollister poured them each a good measure of whiskey, saying, "Had this brought out from Tennessee. Best whiskey there is."

Lucas took a sip and had to agree. It was very smooth. "I sure won't argue that point."

Hollister sat down at his desk. Now that they were cleaned up and had food in their bellies, he was anxious to hear the man's story and said so. "My name is Hollister Evans and I own this ranch. I'd be much obliged if you will tell me your name and the story of how you showed up at my ranch in the condition you did. I'm all ears."

Lucas leaned back in the big, leather chair, took a sip of the whiskey, sighed, and began.

It had been two weeks since Lucas told Hollister his story and he was getting anxious to leave. He told Hollister he had a small amount of gold, still buried up at his place, and would willingly pay for the three horses, the clothes, and the supplies, he'd provided, but the big rancher just laughed and said, "You don't owe me a thing, son. I've enjoyed having you here, and I don't need your gold. Use it to get a new start. But what I would really like, is a Bearskin rug to go in my office. Now, if you could bring me one of those, it would make us even."

"It might take a while, but you've got yourself a deal," Lucas said, sticking out his hand, thanking him again for his hospitality and friendship. We will be back, he assured Hollister and his daughter.

TEN

After stopping in Denver to get the wagon loaded with furniture and tools, they left Denver the same day they got there. Both he and Crying Dove had seen enough of Denver and were anxious to get back.

A cold wind chilled them to the bone as they pulled into the place Lucas called home. With the cabin being burned to the ground, and nothing but a bare spot where it had been, it looked lonely and desolate. "There's a cave up above here, maybe a quarter of a mile or so. We can stay there until I get a new cabin built," he said, urging the wagon toward the barn.

Crying Dove, who was sitting next to him, said, "Until, we, can get the cabin built. I am your woman now, and I will do my share of the work."

Lucas urged the mules on, a little faster, whistling a happy tune. He was a lucky man to have found, Crying Dove.

They worked long days, trying to get enough trees cut and the limbs trimmed off as they built the walls for the new cabin. Lucas laid out the cabin by staking rope in the shape he wanted. There would be five rooms this time, instead of one. This one would be almost four times the size of the old cabin. He was not just building a new cabin – he was building a home for him and Crying Dove, and maybe...? He didn't even want to say the word, in case it would jinx it.

On one hand, Lucas would like to have a son, but on the other side of the coin was the fact that half-breeds were not accepted in the western towns and the problems it would cause were too numerous to count.

He dovetailed the ends of the logs with his axe, and together, he and Crying Dove hefted them into place, leaving only small cracks to be filled with a mixture of mud and grass to seal the walls from the wind and rain.

When the walls were finished, Lucas and Crying Dove stood back and admired their work. "This will be the nicest home anywhere in the mountains," Crying Dove declared.

During all of this, the cave gave them warmth from the ever-increasing cold weather. It was close to thirty feet deep and twenty feet wide – with headroom for a man six feet tall to walk around, comfortably. Unnoticed in the past, small veins of gold showed in the walls that Lucas chipped away at - filling one of his leather tote bags. Water came out of the mountainside, twenty feet or so from the cave and fed the stream not far from where they were building the new cabin.

Impressed by the shower tank the rancher, Hollister Evans had built, Lucas set about building one inside the cave, that he could build a fire under, and heat the water for bathing. He built it out of stone, and lined it with tree sap to keep water from leaking out. It was small, taking ten buckets of water to fill it, but big enough for them to stay clean if they showered together – which Lucas found, he enjoyed very much.

He had built the stall out of timber and there was a small, rock lined trench that fed the used water outside the cave, so the rest of the floor stayed dry.

He'd also built a temporary wall out of leftover material that covered the front of the cave to keep the cold wind and sometimes, rain that came down in torrents.

Lucas entered the cave and stopped for a moment to allow his eyes to get accustomed to the dimmer light.

Even with the light from the fire and the candles Crying Dove had made from the tallow from the animals he'd killed to provide meat and skins to tan, it was still darker than outside.

When his eyes were adjusted, he looked around and saw Crying Dove standing next to the shower tank. She was completely naked and just the sight of her caused Lucas' heart to beat faster.

During their evening meal of deer meat and a variety of edibles Crying Dove found in the forest, she looked across the fire and said, "I believe we need to get the roof on the new cabin as quickly as we can. There is a storm coming."

Lucas shook his head in wonder. The wind had gotten colder, yes, but there was not a dark cloud in the sky, anywhere to be seen, yet this woman could tell there was a storm coming. How she could make such predictions, he had not the slightest idea. He had lived in the mountains for a good many years and he still had no idea of how to predict the weather until he saw actual signs.

"I'll start cutting the timber we'll need, first thing in the morning," he told her. Don't worry, we have plenty of time."

Crying Dove smiled, but said nothing – even though she knew better. The first storm of the season would be a big one and would arrive within a week – not enough time to get the roof completed, but they would try.

For the next two days, Lucas cut down, tall, but small diameter trees that would make the rafters for the roof, while Crying Dove trimmed the branches from them. By the end of the second day, Lucas said, "Tomorrow, we'll put up the rafters, then I'll start cutting down some trees to make the planks for the roof covering, while you gather sap to seal them together. Once that is done, I'll cut the shingles while you put them on, and hope we can finish before that storm you talked about, gets here.

Crying Dove looked at the sky and sniffed the air. The roof would take another four days to finish and she knew they had only three before the storm hit their part of the world. "We need to work longer each day if we are to make it," she informed Lucas, who shrugged his shoulders and said, "Then I guess that's what we'll do."

Lucas' hands, shoulders and back, ached from cutting down trees, then laying them out and turning them into planks that could be nailed to the rafters. It was hard, tedious work, but Lucas believed what Crying Dove told him about the storm coming. In the past she had made predictions and had never been wrong.

Late in the third day, after the sun had gone down and the moon was high in the sky, he and Crying Dove stepped back and admired their work. The walls were up and sealed, and they had just finished the roof. The openings for the doors and windows still needed covering, but other than that, the exterior of the cabin, or log house, as they now called it, was complete.

With leftover branches, they covered the window holes and the two, door openings, then went to the cave for some much-needed rest. They were so tired they didn't bother showering or eating anything.

When morning came, Lucas woke up with sore muscles and shivering from the cold temperature inside the cave.

He quickly dressed then built a fire and put coffee on to boil. Outside, he could hear the wind whistling, and went to the opening in the wall and pulled back the covering . He jumped back as the wind blew snow in his face, which was piled up close to three feet in the opening.

After recovering from his shock, Lucas could see the large snowflakes coming down and being blown this way and that by the wind. The storm Crying Dove had predicted, was upon them, and just when she said it would. He closed the opening and went over to the fire and pulled up one of the two, homemade chairs he'd built, and sat down, feeling the heat.

He looked over at the still sleeping Crying Dove and grinned. She had worked as hard as any man, not only to help build their new home, but had made sure the cave was kept clean, along with cooking their meals. And she never complained when he was feeling passionate.

During all his years of living alone up in the mountains, he'd thought he was happy being alone and away from the world of man, but since having Crying Dove here with him, he knew he had been wrong. Man could survive living by himself. And he could convince himself that's the way he wanted it. But if he were to be completely truthful, the companionship of a good woman was what it took to make living up here, a life to be envied.

He was enjoying his morning cup of coffee when Crying Dove stirred and sat up. She sat up and rubbed her eyes, then looked at Lucas and said, "Why have you let me sleep so late? There is still much work to do. We need coverings for the doorways and windows."

Lucas grinned and said, "With all the hard work you've been doing, I figured you were due for a vacation and some rest. So, I let that storm you've been talking about, come in. There's at least three feet of snow on the ground with more on the way."

Crying Dove leaped to her feet and ran to the doorway and opened it, then stood, looking out across the snow-covered ground.

She closed the door, then turned and looked at Lucas. "Maybe from now on, you will listen to me when I tell you something I know to be true, even though there is no evidence of it, yet."

"When have I never listened to you?" Lucas told her with a broad smile. "Come and sit next to me and have a cup of coffee, while we plan on what to do while we are confined to this cave."

That year, the high country of Colorado saw one of the longest and worse winters it had seen in several years. One storm after another came down on them and being confined to the cave began to grind on their patience.

They never actually argued, but after a while, they kept their own council for long periods of time.

Somewhere during their fourth month of confinement, Crying Dove realized what was happening to them and decided to do something about it before they got to the point of disliking each other.

For breakfast that morning, she made him fried cakes with the last of the dried strawberries in them and the last of the syrup to pour over them.

Lucas looked across the fire at her and could see something in her eyes he hadn't seen in some time – a combination of love, and sadness.

"You made me a special breakfast this morning, and I appreciate it, but from the look on your face I get the feeling something is wrong. Are you feeling all right?"

he asked, even though he knew the answer. Being couped up here in the cave with nowhere to go and the food and water dwindling, was enough to make anyone go nuts.

Without saying a word, Crying Dove stood up, walked over and knelt next to Lucas and then, reached down and kissed him, passionately. And when she released him, she said, "I love you, Lucas Penny and I want us to be friends, again."

"What are you talking about? We're friends," Lucas said, but inside, knew exactly what she meant.

"Do not play coy with me, Lucas Penny. You know exactly what I am talking about. With nowhere to go and nothing to do, we are becoming broody and saying little to each other. While we do not fight, we do not laugh together, either. I want us to laugh, again."

Lucas grinned for the first time in a long time, then stood up and said, said, "Take my hand."

And when she did, he led her to the door and opened it. The sun was shining brightly and even though there was a good two feet of snow on the ground, a good portion of it had melted.

The sky was clear for the first time in months and the temperature had risen to just ten below zero.

Wading into the knee-deep snow, Crying Dove laughingly asked, "Are you crazy? Do you not realize it is freezing cold out here? What are we doing out here?"

"We, my lady, are going to build a snowman," Lucas told her.

She got a strange look on her face and asked, "What is a snowman and what is his purpose? Is he to guard our cave?"

Lucas thought for a moment, then said, "Yes. That is exactly what he is to do. So, he must be big and strong to scare away any attacking Indians or other creatures who come to do us harm."

Not understanding all of the white man's ways, she helped build a giant snowman a short distance from the entrance to their cave. They laughed and threw snowballs at each other, until at last, they were nearly frozen and exhausted.

Crying Dove brought out berries for the eyes, small stones for his nose and mouth while Lucas made a stick into something that looked like a rifle, which he placed in the snowman's arms.

"There… Now we are protected by our new guard," Lucas told Crying Dove.

"And what shall we name him?" she asked.

"Name him?" Lucas asked. "Why does he need a name? Why can't we just call him, the guard?"

With her lips pouted and a sad look in her eyes, Crying Dove said, "No. That will not do. He needs a name."

"Alfonse. We shall call him, Alfonse. My teacher in prep-school was called Alfonse."

Crying Dove threw a snowball at Lucas that hit him in the chest. "That is no name for a fierce guard."

"Then you name him," Lucas told her.

She thought for a moment, then said, "We will call him, Aki Chita, which means Warrior who protects our camp."

"Well now, that's a good name for him," Lucas told her as he took her hand and pulled her to him, kissing her, softly on the lips. "I'm sorry I've been out of sorts. I'll try hard to not let it happen, again."

"Come," she said, "Let us go inside and hide under the blankets where it is warm and we can comfort one another."

They had just reached the entryway to the cave when they heard the scream and saw an arrow lodge itself in the wall, not far from Crying Dove's head.

"Quick, get inside, and toss me my rifle," Lucas told her as he shoved her toward the doorway.

Lucas cursed himself for coming outside without a weapon, which was one of the first rules of being a mountain man. Never go anywhere without something to fight with.

Lucas' rifle came flying out of the opening and he caught it with one hand just as another arrow nearly pierced his head. He dropped to one knee, to be partially hidden by the snow, then looked for movement.

He didn't have to wait long until he saw the Sioux brave step out from behind a tree and raise his bow to fire another arrow.

Lucas threw the butt of his rifle to his shoulder, took a quick aim, then pulled the trigger. There was a loud boom and in the blink of an eye, he saw the brave knocked backward.

Lucas stayed on his knee and waited – his eyes scanning the trees, looking for any movement that would tell him of more Indians, but he saw none.

After a short time, Lucas heard Crying Dove's loud whisper. "Lucas? Are you alright?"

Lucas called out over his shoulder, also in a loud whisper. "Yes, but stay inside. I do not know if we're safe, yet."

With Indians you never knew. They had more patience than all the saints in heaven. There could be several more out there, all still watching and waiting.

Lucas looked at the new repeating rifle Hollister Evans had given him, saying, "You might need this where you're going. I hope it serves you well." It had, so far.

Lucas had been in the same position for nearly an hour and he felt the cold running through him. The sun in the west was throwing long shadows across the snow-covered ground. He was having a hard time keeping his teeth from chattering, and was almost ready to give up and go inside, when he saw just the slightest of movement.

As a young man, trying to learn the ways of the mountain man, an old-timer told him, "Son, if you want to keep your hair, don't never stare at anything in particular. Look at everything like it was a huge picture. And take close notice of everything in that there picture so that if anything becomes out of place, it stands out like ah sore thumb."

And that's what was happening right now. The picture had changed. Where a shoulder and head hadn't been a few seconds ago, was there now. The second Indian was peeking his head around from behind the tree.

Lucas eased the butt of the rifle to his shoulder, as he sighted on the man's head and when he was sure, he squeezed the trigger.

The rifle's sound reverberated through the forest like a canon going off and when Lucas looked again, there was no Indian to be seen.

Again, he crouched and waited until darkness was upon him. Then, when he felt it was safe, he moved back - and quietly entered the cave.

The blast of warmth almost made him cry – he was that cold. Crying Dove helped him over to the fire and sat him down in one of the chairs, then draped a blanket over his shoulders, and tried to give him a cup of hot, coffee, but he was trembling too badly, and his hands were too stiff to hold the cup.

Crying Dove held the coffee cup to his lips and he took small sips, feeling the hot liquid spread throughout his insides.

Little by little Lucas Penny came back. His shivering ceased and he was finally able to hold the coffee cup.

When Crying Dove was satisfied Lucas would be all right, she brought him a small bowl of steaming hot, stew. "There is more if you want it, but you should go slow."

Lucas nodded his head and watched as Crying Dove picked up his rifle and left the cave. He ate his stew, slowly, and waited.

By the time Lucas finished the second bowl of stew and Crying Dove had not returned, he was becoming concerned. She hadn't said why she was going out, but whatever her reason, she should be back by now.

He checked and loaded his pistol, then pulled on his coat and went to the door and was opening it when a flaming arrow struck the brush wall. He jerked it out and put out the fire with a handful of snow before it could spread.

The Indian's voice filled the quiet air and Lucas jerked his head in that direction, drawing his pistol.

"White man! I have your woman... but it is you I want. You killed two of my brothers, and you must pay."

"You and your friends fired at me, first. I only defended myself. If I am a stronger warrior than you it is only because the gods willed it so. Send my woman back and I will not have to kill you, too," Lucas called out, looking for any movement, but saw none.

"Step out where I can see you," Lucas said. "Only a coward hides behind the skirt of a woman!"

Crying Dove was shoved out from behind a tree, a short distance in front of where Lucas stood. She had a knife against her throat.

"You speak of courage, white man, and of the gods protecting you. Will they protect you if you fight with me, man to man? Or are you afraid to face my knife?"

In the moonlight it's difficult to make out features even from a short distance, and because the Indian was covered by a bearskin coat, Lucas couldn't make out the tribe the Indian was from, but he could read the smugness in his face and voice.

"What say you, white man? Will you face Diving Crow?"

Before Lucas could answer, he saw snow fall from the ledge above the cave and looked up in time to see two braves leaping at him with knives in their hands. He stepped to the side, causing one of the braves to land face first in the snow, but not fast enough to avoid the second one.

The brave landed on him, taking both of them to the ground. Lucas felt the pain of the brave's knife as it dug into his left shoulder.

As they went down, Lucas pulled his pistol and stuck it against the brave's chest and pulled the trigger. The force of the shot pushed the brave to the side, allowing Lucas to roll over and shoot the second brave, who was now on his knees, with his knife raised in the air, ready to drive the blade into Lucas.

The bullet tore into the Indian's forehead, knocking him over backward.

At the same time Lucas was doing battle with the two braves, Crying Dove was not about to be left out of the fracas. When the two braves leaped from the ledge above the cave, Crying Dove shoved Diving Crow's knife away from her throat and bit down on his wrist, while at the same time, stomping down on his nearly frozen foot.

He dropped his knife – let out a scream, jerked his wrist from Crying Dove's teeth and ran off into the forest, yelling over his shoulder, "You will pay for this, white man!"

Lucas and Crying Dove carried the two dead braves away from the cave and laid them next to the other two.

"Sioux," Crying Dove stated, matter of factly. "Why would the Sioux be trying to kill you?"

"It happened a couple of springs ago. I had a couple of run-ins with them over my hunting on what they consider, their territory. Unfortunately, several of them died in the process," Lucas said as he took Crying Dove by the hand and led her back to the cave.

When morning came, they went up to see about the dead bodies, but stopped short. They were too late. The meat eaters had already been there and what was left wasn't pretty.

"Not even enough left for the Sioux to come and take away," Lucas said, shaking his head.

Even so, they did what they could to place all the remains in one spot and spent close to five hours, hunting down rocks underneath the snow, with which to cover the bones of the four braves.

Spring came suddenly, without warning. One morning when they got up, the sky was clear, the sun was shining brightly and the snow was melting. The air was crisp, but not cold, and filled their nostrils with joy.

Lucas tore down the temporary wall that covered the front of the cave to let it air out. Having been walled in for several months, the inside smelled like smoke and stale, damp air.

"Today we will enjoy the day, and tomorrow, we will move into the cabin and we will begin making it a home," Lucas said with a broad smile.

And so, it began – the process of making a home out of their newly built cabin. While Lucas brought everything from the wagon and set it in place, including an iron bed frame. Crying Dove sewed material together for their mattress and filled it with dry grass, then sewed several skins together to make a blanket – along with searching in the forest for herbs and other edibles. She also found plants to make healing potions from and stored them in a bag and placed them on a shelf Lucas had put up in the cooking area, which he called, the kitchen.

Lucas' biggest challenge was the cast iron cook stove and the tall stove pipe that led up to, and through the ceiling. When he was finished, he stood back and admired his work.

By now, she had learned to speak the white man's language very fluently, while Lucas had learned to speak, Arapahoe. One would speak in Arapahoe and the other would answer in English, then vice-versa.

One morning, Lucas was coming out of the barn and saw a deer staring at him. He was so close; Lucas didn't need his rifle. He very slowly, drew his pistol and shot the deer – then looked at the sky and said, "Thank you."

Crying Dove was overjoyed when she saw Lucas come walking up to the front of the cabin with a deer over his shoulders. They desperately needed the meat.

A week after moving into the cabin, Lucas had gone off in search of an elk to take care of their low meat supply. Deer meat was all right, but it didn't last nearly as long as an elk.

Crying Dove danced around the kitchen, singing one of her native songs, in her native tongue. Life was good. She had a wonderful home to live in, food in the larder, her health was good and she had a man who adored her. What more could a woman want, she wondered?

Suddenly she stopped and stared at the window. It came to her like a lightning bolt. She wanted a child. Yes… she wanted a son for Lucas. They had discussed it while they were living in the cave and Lucas had danced around the subject, saying it would be nice to have a child, but if they didn't, that would be all right, too, as long as he had her.

She hadn't believed that, then, and she didn't believe that now. Something inside her told her, Lucas wanted a son he could train to hunt and fish and do all the things a young man needed to know.

In Crying Dove's mind, he would grow up to be tall and strong and he would stand against anyone who tried to overpower him. He would become a man to be proud of.

Suddenly the door to the cabin was swung open and Diving Crow and six other braves came inside, bows and arrows drawn.

Crying Dove stopped her singing and dancing and stared at the Sioux braves. "If you are looking for my husband, he is not here and I do not know how long he will be gone, so, leave! You are not welcome here!" she said in the Sioux language.

Diving Crow nodded to his braves and they searched the interior of the cabin and came back, shaking their heads, no. "He is not here," one of them said.

Diving Crow's eyes showed the anger inside him. He had expected to catch the white man unaware so he could take his time, torturing him to a long, painful death, making him beg to be killed.

But once again the gods had spared him and Diving Crow was angry. He looked at Crying Dove and an idea began to take shape in his mind.

"If I cannot find this man who invades my land, then I shall make him come to me," he told his friends.

Crying Dove didn't need to have it explained to her, to know that she was in trouble. If she was to die, she would not go, quietly.

She grabbed the handle of the pot of boiling water sitting on the stove and threw it in their direction, hearing screams of pain. She then pulled a large knife from where it hung on the wall and faced Diving Crow, who had not been hit with the boiling water.

Five of the six braves ran out of the cabin and headed for the nearby creek in the hope of stopping the pain of their burned skin.

The sixth of the braves stepped up next to Diving Crow and said, "I will help you with the squaw."

Diving Crow raised his hand and said, "Only if I need help – which I will not. Go and see about our brothers while I take care of this, she-wolf."

"As you wish, brother," he said and left the cabin.

Crying Dove held the knife out in front of her, saying, "Leave with your friend. I do not want to kill you, but I will if you try to harm me."

Diving Crow leaned his head back and laughed. "I like a squaw who fights back. It makes the taking much more enjoyable."

At that moment, Crying Dove was more afraid than she had ever been in her entire life. She swallowed and said, "Sing your death song, stupid brave. For if you try, it will be the last thing you ever do." She was trying to sound brave and unafraid, but inside, she was filled with the knowledge that unless she was very lucky, or Lucas suddenly appeared, she was about to die.

Diving Crow could see the defiance in her eyes but with him being nearly twice her size, he let his bravado get the best of him, and leaped at her.

She fought him like a wildcat, slashing at him with her knife and cutting him in several places. But still he came at her with a vengeance. At one point he hit her alongside the head and sent her reeling across the room. The pain was excruciating and tears ran down her face, but the fear of dying was strong enough in her to let her regain her balance and face him, not willing to give in.

"You fight well for a woman, but I'm beginning to tire of this game we play." And with that, he threw a chair at her and followed it, driving his fist into her stomach. He then jerked the knife from her hand and slapped her along the side of her face.

She was knocked to the floor but somehow, got to her feet and ran for the door. But he was too fast and tackled her, taking both of them to the floor.

****

Lucas rode into the yard with a big smile on his face, calling out, "Hello the house. Your man is home with an elk!"

When the door remained shut and there was no answer, he called out, again. "Crying Dove, it is me, Lucas and I have meat…"

And when there still was no answer, he jumped off his horse and headed toward the door, stopping just short of it. There, as plain as anything he'd ever seen, was moccasin tracks. Several sizes – which meant more than one Indian had come and gone.

With his blood soaring with panic, he ran inside the cabin and stopped. The furniture was broken into pieces and the interior looked like an enraged bull buffalo had been trapped inside the cabin.

He swallowed and said, "Crying Dove?"

From near the back door, he faintly heard his name being called. 'Lu… Lucas…"

Lucas ran to the back of the cabin and there, curled into a ball, lay Crying Dove – and when she looked up at him, her eyes were swollen almost closed and her face was covered with blood. Her lips were so swollen she could hardly speak.

Lucas dropped to his knees and said, "Shh, don't try to talk. Not now. Later when you are feeling better."

And with that, he picked her up in his arms and took her into the bedroom, and stopped. Not only had the bed frame been destroyed, but the mattress had been ripped apart.

Lucas laid her down, gently, then scrounged around until he found the fur blanket, she'd made. He took it in and laid it in front of the fireplace, then built a fire and put some water on to heat.

When this was done, he went back into the bedroom and lifted Crying Dove into his arms and held her close, kissing her on the head. "You're going to be all right," he whispered.

He felt her body stiffen. "No, I will never be all right, again," she said through her puffed up lips.

Not liking what was going through his mind right then, Lucas tried to laugh it off and said, "Of course you will. I will clean you up and you'll see, in a few days you'll feel as good as new, again."

Tears ran down her face, mixing with the dried blood that dripped off her chin. She shook her head and said, "No. I am no longer worthy of being called Lucas Penny's woman."

Gritting his teeth, trying not to scream out, Lucas laid Crying Dove on the blanket and said, "You are my woman, now and forever. Nothing will ever change that."

Crying Dove looked up at him and said, "But they…"

Lucas put his hand to her lips and said, "Shh. You are safe now. Rest, while I fix you something to eat so you can regain your strength."

Crying Dove said nothing. She closed her eyes, feeling the warmth of the fire and was soon, sound asleep. Somewhere in her deep slumber, she felt a warm, wet cloth being wiped against her face and other parts of her body, but she was too deep into sleep to wake up or respond. The warm cloth felt good against her bruised skin.

Crying Dove slept for nearly twenty hours and when her eyes finally opened, the first thing she saw was Lucas sitting in a chair, looking at her.

When she tried to sit up, she felt pain radiating throughout her body and the memory came flooding back. She slumped back down with Lucas following her, running his hand over her face, saying, "Welcome back, sleepy-head. You've been asleep for a long time, so it might take a little while to come back."

"I need to get up," she told him and when Lucas realized what she meant, he helped her to her feet.

On wobbly legs Crying Dove made her way out the back door and into the woods. The movement and fresh air helped her feel better, physically, but not mentally. She knew what he'd said, but what if he never looked at her the same? Or, what if he did and because of what happened, she could never bear him a child?

When she went back into the house, she was able to take a better look at the inside of the cabin and was surprised to see that everything had been repaired and the house looked very much like it did before Diving Crow and his friends came.

When he'd built the new log cabin, he had installed a well inside the house, and a shower like the one in the cave. In fact, it was the one from the cave, only with improvements.

"Come," he said to Crying Dove, holding out his hand.

And when she gave him her hand, he led her to the shower area, slowly undressed her and himself, then guided the two of them into the steaming hot water.

During the shower, and his gentleness, something happened to Crying Dove and she told Lucas everything that happened, leaving nothing out.

Lucas had guessed it had been Diving Crow, but had waited for her to tell him. He had wanted to go after him and make him pay, from the moment he found her on the floor, but reluctantly decided to wait until she was on her feet, again.

That night, lying in bed beside her, he listened to the small snores that escaped her mouth and smiled. She was going to be all right, and so was he, but not before he made Diving Crow and his friends pay for what they'd done.

Another thought crept into his mind. He knew none of the traps he'd set around the cabin had been activated because he knew the way through them. But why hadn't the braves who had raided the cabin? He would check them in the morning.

The following morning, before Crying Dove woke up, Lucas slipped out of the cabin and in the early morning light, he saw why they hadn't been injured. A wide area leading up to the front of the cabin was filled with traps that had their teeth clamped around sticks.

That day, Lucas spent a good portion of the day, resetting the traps, both in front of the cabin and over in front of the cave, plus, digging some holes and planting pointed stakes in them, then covering them with brush, grass and leaves.

When he was finished, he looked out across the area and if he didn't know where the holes with the stakes were, he wouldn't be able to see them. If anyone or anything tried to get to the cabin or the cave and even if they figured out where the steel traps were, he was sure they would find the hole traps, but not to their liking…

ELEVEN

Two days later, Lucas installed Crying Dove, back in the cave, loaded down with water, food, a rifle, a handgun and ammunition - with instructions to stay hidden. "I shouldn't be gone more than a few days, and I want you to be safe," he told her.

"I do not want you to do this," she told him with pleading in her eyes, but he looked down at her and replied, "This is something I have to do."

He knew she was scared and had every right to be, so he took her into his arms and said, "I promise; I won't be gone but a few days."

Lucas wasn't sure what he said was true or not. He had no idea where the Sioux camp was, and even when he found it, how long it would take him to take his revenge. Life up in the high country was different than down in Denver or cities like it. You couldn't go to the sheriff or police and tell them what happened and have the authorities do what needed to be done. Up in the high country, each man was responsible for making his own law.

Actually, this was revenge – pure and simple. Diving Crow and his followers had come into his home and violated his woman, and they had to stand accused and be punished.

Lucas let his sorrel mare pick her way through the trees. He decided against bringing a packhorse. He was traveling light – a rifle, a handgun, a sack filled with ammunition, a water canteen hanging from the pommel of his saddle, a coffee pot, a sack of coffee and a blanket, tied behind the saddle, along with a pair of binoculars he'd gotten from a sergeant who had retired from the army. Lucas had just recently decided to become a mountain man and happened to run onto the sergeant in a saloon. The sergeant had lost his money over a horse race and was flat broke.

He was on a hunting trip, but not the kind he normally did.

He scoured the country for four days, from sunup until sundown without finding a trace of an Indian camp – but late, on the fourth day, riding up onto a large boulder, he was able to see out over a large valley, and there, approximately three miles in a wide clearing next to a good-size stream, was an Indian camp. He didn't know if it was the one he was looking for, but guessed it might be since he hadn't seen any others.

Not far from the camp, Lucas found a place where he could hobble his horse on lush grass so she wouldn't roam too far, then set off, afoot, carrying his rifle – his handgun hanging against his leg. He'd also, taken off his boots and put on a pair of moccasins which would allow him to travel quietly.

Lucas traveled fast down through the forest for about two and a half miles, then slowed down, taking his time to come up on the camp from a place where he could see them without being seen.

One of the reasons Indians kept dogs – other than to eat them in lean times – they made great watchdogs. When anyone who wasn't supposed to be there got close, the dogs would begin to bark, alerting the camp. Lucas could see six of them running around, playing with each other.

Crying Dove had given him a description of the men who had attacked her, but from the distance he was from the camp, they all looked pretty much the same. Lucas took the binoculars out of the case and lay down on his stomach, propping himself up on his elbows. Before putting the binoculars to his eyes, he made sure the lens were not reflecting the sunlight. Sunlight reflecting off the lens of a pair of binoculars can be seen for many miles. All he needed was for them to notice and he would have a whole bunch of Indian braves to deal with.

It took only minutes to spot Diving Crow and he could see the scratches on his face, still not completely healed.

Lucas had to lower the binoculars because he was shaking with anger.

Less than an hour later, after he had calmed down, he put the glasses to his eyes and searched the camp once more.

Luck was with him as he watched Diving Crow and four braves ride out of the camp, heading up the mountain, heading right toward him. They seemed to be in no hurry, so Lucas continued to watch them until he was sure they were not coming to find him, but would pass right by him. Getting to his feet, he hurried back to his horse and led her to the side a short distance - until he found a place where they wouldn't be seen.

With his hand over his horse's nose, Lucas watched from a distance as Diving Crow and his friends rode pass him. He could have killed Diving Crow and wanted to, but then he would have had to deal with the others and that could have been a disaster for him, so he let them pass.

As he watched them ride past him, he recalled an old mountain man who had saved his life shortly after coming into the mountains for the first time. He had definitely been a greenhorn and if it hadn't been for Ezekiel Hackensack, he would not be here today.

Like many others, he'd come into the mountains with his head filled with knowledge he gained from dime novels, thinking he would become wealthy within a few months. It was springtime and he was filled with bravado. The first month, he'd lost the little finger on his left hand from mishandling a beaver trap and almost bled to death.

During the months from spring through summer, he ate up his supplies like they would last forever. When he ran out of meat, he decided to go hunting since he had yet to catch anything in his traps, which he later learned, he was using the wrong kind of bait.

Several miles from his camp, he wandered onto a heard of elk. Thinking how lucky he was, he stepped out in the open and took a shot, missing the elk and scattering them.

What he didn't realize was that he was hunting them during rut and the bull elks weren't too happy about him being there and one of them charged him and when it finished with him, he had to count his lucky stars that he was still among the living. Between being stabbed by the bull elk's antlers, its sharp paws cut through his clothes and broke three ribs, along with leaving his upper torso full of cuts and abrasions. It took him two days to crawl back to his camp, only to find an old man sitting around his campfire, drinking his coffee.

"Praise the Lord, you made it back, pilgrim," was the first words out of the old man's mouth.

Lucas was almost out of his head with pain and the loss of blood made everything look fuzzy.

When the old man saw the extent of Lucas' wounds, he promptly set about trying to save the young man's life.

After doctoring him the best he could, he went off and came back shortly with a deer across his shoulders.

"Here, eat this," the old man said, holding up a piece of raw liver. "You've lost a sight of blood and it needs to be replenished. Eat it. It will help save your life."

Reluctantly, Lucas began to eat the raw liver – blood covering his hands and dripping from his chin. And while Lucas ate, Ezekiel dropped to his knees and began to pray.

Exactly what the old man was saying, Lucas wasn't sure, but knew the man was praying to help save his life.

For several days, Lucas was in and out of his head with delirium and he vaguely remembered being fed soup.

On the morning Lucas returned to the living, the old man looked at him and smiled. "It was nip and tuck there for a while, there, young fella. But between me and the Good Lord, we kept you from the clutches of that demon, Satan, himself."

As the days passed, Lucas learned the man's name – Ezekiel Hackensack – along with the fact that he'd once been a hell-fire and brimstone preacher, who got sick and tired of preaching to people who constantly backslid, and lied about it.

"So, in the end, I came up here in the mountains where I can be closer to God, and not have to listen to those blaspheming heathens. That was nine years ago and I've never been sorry – not even for one day. No-sir, not even for one minute. Me and the Lord converse daily and he provides for me."

They stayed together through the winter and into the late spring when one morning, Ezekiel loaded up his mule and said, "Son, the Good Lord told me this morning that I have taught you all you need to know to survive up here and it's time for me to go."

Lucas remembered asking him why he needed to go?"

"The Almighty's got things planned for me. Don't know what they are, and I ain't gonna ask. I just go where he tells me, just like I did when I found you."

As Ezekiel was riding out of the camp, he called over his shoulder, "When fighting Indians, always remember to have patience, and pick your battles when you can."

For three days Lucas followed Diving Crow and his followers at a safe distance. On the third day he was sure where they were going. They were headed straight for his place, again.

"Oh, the arrogance," Lucas said to himself. Turning his horse off to the left, he put his feet against his horse's sides and felt it pick up speed. "Whether they get caught in one of my traps, or not, they're going to be in for a big surprise."

Lucas rode hard to circle around and get back to the cabin before Diving Crow and his friends arrived.

After tending to his horse and the other horses and the mule in the barn, Lucas knocked on the back door of the cabin, saying, "It's me... Lucas... Coming in." But when he tried, he found it was barred. He was knocking on the door, again when he heard Crying Dove's voice coming to him from behind, saying, "Put your hands on top of your head and turn around, slowly."

And when he did as he was told, Crying Dove let out a huge sigh and ran into his arms.

"I had to be sure," she told him, planting kisses all over his face.

Lucas pushed her away, gently and said, "We need to get inside, quickly. We'll be having visitors in a short while and I want to be ready for them."

As they hurried around to the front door, Crying Dove said, "Surely, you don't mean..."

"That's exactly who I mean. And he has four braves with him."

Suddenly, Crying Dove had fear in her eyes and she stopped moving. Lucas looked over his shoulder and saw her, then spun around and lifted her into his arms, then hurried inside the cabin.

When he set Crying Dove on her feet, he took her by the shoulders and said, "Snap out of it. I can't have you like this when they get here. I need both of us to take care of them."

Crying Dove shook her head back and forth, and said, "I'm sorry. I'm all right, now. What do you want me to do?"

TWELVE

Diving Crow held up his hand as he brought his horse to a stop, then slipped off his horse and stood, looking down at the cabin, several hundred feet beyond him.

The four braves with him, followed suit and one of them stepped up next to him and asked, "When do we attack?"

Diving Crow looked at his friend, Elk Caller, and said, "Do not get in a hurry. This white man is no ordinary white man. He is shrewd and we must take care and plan our attack. First, we do not know if he is in there. We must make sure before doing anything else."

Sleeping Cat was a tall, rawboned brave who could go to sleep almost instantly. All he had to do was close his eyes. But he was also, a fierce warrior and at the moment, wide awake and eager to fight. Diving Crow called him over and told him to check the barn to see if the white man's horse was there. "If he is here, there will be three horses and a mule."

Sleeping Cat just nodded his head and disappeared into the forest.

It took him close to half an hour to make his way to a place where he could observe the backdoor of the barn. His eyes wandered back and forth, looking for any movement and listening for any sounds that would tell him if the man was inside the barn.

When he was satisfied, Sleeping Cat eased himself closer to the barn. He was maybe twenty feet from the back door when he stepped into one of Lucas' hole traps and felt the sharp sticks drive themselves into his right foot. The pain was instant and excruciating, causing him to lose his balance and when he began to fall, he put out his right hand, which landed on one of the beaver traps, causing it to slam closed.

This time, he could not keep from screaming – which was heard by both the Indians and the man and woman inside the cabin.

Lucas grinned. "One down, four to go," he said easing over to one of the rifle ports and peeking outside.

After seeing no one, he stepped back and said, "I do believe the company has arrived and the party is about to start.

Diving Crow and the others jerked their heads in the direction of the sound when they heard Sleeping Cat's soulful cry.

"What has happened to Sleeping Cat?" one of the braves asked.

"I do not know," Diving Crow told him. "But knowing the white man, Sleeping Cat is now with his ancestors."

"How did he know we are here?" one of the remaining braves asked.

"I do not know that, either," Diving Crow said. "It is like I told you, he is a shrewd man with many of the gods on his side. We will wait until the sun is far against the horizon, then we will spread out and make our way close enough to the cabin to send fire arrows into the roof."

The others nodded their heads. It was a good plan. Setting the cabin on fire would force the white man and his squaw out into the open where they could easily kill them.

Lucas and Crying Dove watched through the small peek holes, knowing they would be coming soon.

Lucas was looking through one of the front holes when he saw a brave, bent over, coming toward him. Lucas watched and waited until the brave was inside the trap zone and fired a shot at him, hitting him in the leg.

The brave, fell backward and drove his hand into one of the pit traps, driving the wooden stakes into his hand, and when he tried to roll over, his elbow landed on a beaver trap.

Suddenly, Lucas felt sorry for him. It was a slow, painful way to die. He could hear the brave singing his death song. Sighting down the barrel of his rifle, Lucas took him out of his misery.

Lucas looked over his shoulder and said, "It's time."

Without a word, Crying Dove raced to the ladder placed against the back wall, and climbed it to the trap door in the ceiling – then climbed out onto the roof and lay flat on her stomach, and waited.

Lucas had been burned out, before and as he told Crying Dove during their preparation for the attack, "I'm going to do my best to see that doesn't happen, again."

Crying Dove found twenty, large gourds and they had filled them with water, then placed them in various locations on the roof. If they tried shooting fire arrows onto the roof, they would be ready for them.

When Sparrow Man, the brave Lucas shot, to take him out of his misery, went down, Diving Crow and the two remaining braves pulled back, in among the trees where they could not be seen.

"He truly must have the gods on his side," Cougar, one of the two remaining braves said, shaking his head. "He has killed two more of our brothers and we stand here doing nothing. I say we ride down there and give him a slow, painful death."

Diving Crow looked at Cougar with contempt and said, "Go ahead. But sing your death song as you go because you will die if you do something that stupid."

"What would you have us do?" Cougar asked. "Turn and run like some cowardly coyote?"

Diving Crow bristled up, anger in his eyes. "You of all of my brothers know I am no coward. We have fought, side by side, have we not?"

Cougar knew this was true. Diving Crow was one of the bravest warriors in the tribe, but he was angry and wanted revenge for the deaths of his two comrades. "We have, and I know you to be strong in battle, but what are we to do? The white man sits inside his cabin and kills us as easily as swatting a fly while we stand here and do nothing."

"If we cannot go to him, we must bring him to us," Diving Crow said, at last, as he looked out across the space between himself and the cabin – measuring the distance. "It will be a long shot, but I think we can do it."

Lucas had seen them move back, in among the tress, and came to the conclusion that he needed a better position to shoot from. He filled his pockets with ammunition, then climbed onto the roof and lay flat, just below the roofline, where he had a much better view. He could lay his rifle on the top edge of the roof to allow him a better shot.

Crying Dove crawled over and lay next to him. "What is happening?"

Without taking his eyes off the spot where the Indians disappeared, he said, "They realize they can't rush the cabin without getting killed, so, I'm guessing they will try to burn the cabin down."

Crying Dove looked at the distance between the cabin and the forest and said, "It is a long way from here to the forest. Do you think they can shoot fire arrows that far?"

"If they have strong bows and if the angle is right? It's possible," Lucas said, eyeing the distance.

Crying Dove smiled. "But from up here, you will have a clear shot at them and it is not too far for a rifle shot."

Lucas nodded his head. "That's about the size of it."

Just inside the tree line, Diving Crow built a small fire and they used pieces of cloth, torn from Walks Softly's shirt, to wrap the tips of the arrows they hoped would set fire to the roof of the cabin.

When they were ready, Diving Crow said, "It is doubtful if he can shoot us from inside the cabin. The angle is not right. But in case he gets lucky, we will all step out and fire our arrows at the same time. He cannot shoot all three of us."

"Now," Diving Crow said, and the three braves stepped out and raised their bows.

At the same time - a shot rang out and Walks Softly was knocked backwards, his arrow flying harmlessly into the sky.

Crying Dove watched as two, flaming arrows arched their way across the sky and landed on the lower part of the roof.

Without hesitation, Crying Dove leaped to her feet and made her way down to the burning arrows and poured water on them, then hurried back to where Lucas lay, sighting down the barrel.

Just as she dropped down beside him, she heard the second roar of the rifle and looked toward the forest in time to see another of the braves, go down.

Diving Crow dragged Cougar inside the tree line, then knelt down next to him. Blood was seeping from his mouth as he choked out his death song.

Diving Crow could see there was nothing he could do for his friend, so, he laid his hand on Cougar's chest and said, "You die a true warrior, my friend. I will sing your praises."

Cougar looked up at Diving Crow and tried to speak, but nothing came out. He closed his eyes, gave a shudder and went to his happy hunting grounds.

Diving Crow, then dragged Walks Softly inside the trees and lay him next to Cougar. There were still two of his friends to go after, but Diving Crow knew if he tried, he was a dead man. He wasn't afraid to die, but to do so, needlessly, would be stupid. If he died, who would take his friends back for a proper burial. But how was he to do that with the white man and his rifle waiting for him to show himself?

Diving Crow was livid with anger. The white man had beat him, again. After some thought, he walked to the edge of the tree line and called out, "You have won, this time, white man, but we will meet again, I promise you. But now, I need to reclaim my brothers so they may have a proper burial. Will you allow me to come and get them?"

Lucas thought for a moment. If he allowed Diving Crow to come in and try to take his friends out, he would more than likely step into one of the hole traps or step on a beaver trap, which in the end, would rid him of the man.

But on the other side of the coin, he felt he should allow him to gather his friends and give them proper burials, it was the right thing to do.

"I declare a temporary peace between us. I will bring your friends to you and allow you to take them away. If I do this, we will not try to kill each other. Once you are gone, the truce will be over and if I see you, again, I will send you to be with your friends," Lucas called out.

As much as he wanted the white man dead, he knew if he wanted to take his friends with him, he would have to consent to the truce. "You have my word, white man."

As Lucas stood up, Crying Dove stood up, too, and laid her hand on his shoulder. "Do you think you can trust him?"

He looked down at her and said, "As you know, being an Indian, it is bad luck for an Indian to break his word – especially with something like this. So, yes, I think I can trust him, but just to make sure, I think you should come along and cover him with a rifle."

Lucas and Crying Dove went to the barn and got the mule to haul the dead bodies. He was adjugated from all the shooting and screaming, but when Lucas gently rubbed his forehead and spoke softly to him, he calmed down.

First, they retrieved the brave from in front of the cabin and when they got close, the mule reacted to the smell of blood. He began snorting and bucking until Lucas calmed him down, again.

Once the brave was draped over the mule's back, they went to the back of the barn where they found the brave sitting upright, blood running from his wrist and ankle.

When he saw the white man and the squaw approaching him, even though his strength was almost gone, with his good hand he gripped his knife, ready to fight.

Lucas raised his hand, palm forward and said, "We come in peace. I am to take you back to your friend so he can take you back to your tribe."

When Sleeping Cat hesitated, Crying Dove spoke up. "It is true. All but one of your friends are dead and we have made a truce with the one left, to bring you and this other one," she said, pointing at the dead Indian lying across the mule's back, "to him so he can take you and the others back to your people so he can bury the ones who died here, today."

Still, he held the knife in the fighting position. He did not trust the white man or the squaw with him, so he did not relinquish his knife. With what little strength he had, he called out, "Diving Crow – do you have a peace agreement with the white man for him to bring me to you?"

Diving Crow was happy to hear Sleeping Cat's voice, even if it did sound weak, and he called, back, "Yes. For now, we are at peace, but only so I can have my brothers back with me. Allow him to bring you to me."

Crying Dove ran into the barn and returned with two pieces of leather strap – which she tied around Sleeping Cat's bleeding wrist and ankle.

"Hopefully you have not already lost too much blood. Hopefully, this will allow you to get back to your people where they can tend to you," Crying Dove told him.

Sleeping Cat stared at the squaw, not knowing what to make of her trying to save his life?

With Lucas' help, Sleeping Cat was hoisted onto the back of the mule.

Diving Crow watched as the white man and the squaw came up to him and stopped. The fact that the squaw had her rifle trained on him did not go unnoticed. He pointed toward her and said, "She does not need that. I am an honorable man and will do as I have agreed."

Crying Dove lowered the rife, but still kept an eye on Diving Crow's every move.

Together, Lucas and Diving Crow loaded the three dead braves onto their horses and tied them in place, then helped Sleeping Cat onto the back of his horse.

Diving Crow swung up onto his steed and looked down at Lucas. "Remember this, white man, the raging blood of my body seeks revenge, and I will not stop until I have it. So, keep looking behind you, for one day, I will be there, and you will die."

Without another word, Diving Crow swung his horse - leading the other four, rode away.

THIRTEEN

The air was turning cold. The skies were indicating snow was on the way. Lucas had shot a bear and an elk to see them through the coming winter and was in the barn, working on the skins – the elk skin would be used for clothing, while the bear skin would be tanned and taken down to Hollister Evans, the rancher who had helped them in their time of need.

Lucas was busy at work when he heard Crying Dove call out, "I am going into the woods to find the last of the berries and other things before the snow comes."

"Do you want me to go with you?" Lucas called back.

"No, I will be fine. Finish preparing the bearskin rug for your rancher, friend. It is late in the season, so I won't be gone long."

And with that, Crying Dove walked into the forest, looking for anything she could find that would help see them through the coming cold time.

Tanning hides is slow, tedious work and Lucas allowed time to slip away from him before he wondered why he hadn't heard Crying Dove's voice, telling him she had returned. He hung the bear skin on the wall of the barn, washed his hands in a bucket of water, then went to the cabin, calling out, "Crying Dove," as he walked in the back door.

It was late in the afternoon and she should have been in the kitchen, preparing their evening meal, but the cabin was empty – and no heat coming from the cook stove.

He searched the entire cabin, then went outside and looked around. He could plainly see her tracks leading into the forest, but none coming back.

Suddenly, Lucas felt the fear filling him. He ran into the cabin and strapped on his pistol, then took his rifle from the pegs it was lying on, and raced outside.

He looked at the ground and saw the direction the moccasins went, and followed them.

Once he was inside the forest, her tracks were not as easy to follow, but there were other signs; a broken twig, ruffled leaves and such that allowed Lucas to follow her trail.

Lucas came to an abrupt stop and stared down at the basket, laying on its side. There was no doubt, it belonged to Crying Dove, of that, he was sure.

He looked around, taking a close look at the area around him. There had been a scuffle. Someone had overtaken her and she had put up a fight. There, on a pile of leaves was a small amount of blood. But the question was, whose blood, was it?

Diving Crow! The man's name pounded into his brain like a cannon shot.

Once he calmed his nerves down, Lucas realized he couldn't definitely know it was Diving Crow who'd done this. A few weeks back, he'd seen signs of a group of Lakota in the area and if they found a woman in the woods, they would have taken her as a slave or to be traded for whatever there was to be traded for.

Trying to think rationally, Lucas went back to the barn and saddled the roan, mare. He considered taking the mule and supplies, but decided against it. They would slow him down. By now, it was night and dark clouds filled the sky, making it impossible for him to find or follow any tracks.

That night, Lucas Penny got very little sleep as he paced the floor.

At first light, Lucas rode into the forest and stopped at the place where the basket still lay on its side, and let his eyes roam over the area. Satisfied, he followed the tracks of a horse with a heavy burden.

Whoever took her - they were riding double, which in Lucas' mind meant, they had possibly come up on her, accidental.

On the late afternoon of the second day, snow began to fall.

Lucas stopped under the limbs of a pine tree and cursed his luck. The tracks had been elusive at best, and now with snow covering the ground, any sign would be lost.

"No matter. I will go on," he told himself as he urged the roan forward.

It was another two days before he topped out over a ridge and sat looking out over the forest. There! It was not much more than a whisper of smoke trailing into the sky, but without a doubt, it was smoke!

Lucas studied the land and decided it was still another day's ride, away. He urged the roan forward, excitement building up inside him.

Once he was down in the lower part of the mountain, he could no longer see the smoke, but continued riding in the general direction – hoping to pick up the smell.

The following morning, before the sun was directly overhead, the roan's ears perked up and Lucas pulled her to a halt.

He slid from her back and listened carefully. Sure enough, he heard the sounds of horses running and people yelling, along with the smell of smoke he'd been searching for.

After ground hitching his horse so she could crop grass, Lucas made his way toward the noise, fear beginning to fill him, once again. With people yelling and horses running, it could only be a couple of things. They could be practicing for a raid, which he doubted. His greatest fear was they were the ones who'd captured Crying Dove and had her tied to a post, torturing her to death. It was one of the things they liked to do.

When he got too close to stay upright for fear of being seen, Lucas crawled on his belly to a spot where he could observe what was going on.

He looked down into the camp and was surprised to see Diving Crow tied to a post with arrows sticking out of him. He was dead – his body hanging, limp, with blood dripping onto the ground. Lakota braves continued to ride past Diving Crow, firing arrows into his body.

Momentarily relieved, Lucas looked around, his eyes searching for any sign of Crying Dove.

There, on the far side of the camp, he could see the naked body of a woman, lying on the ground, stretched out on her back, spread eagle, tied to stakes, and women and children, kicking her and beating her with sticks.

He didn't have to see her up close to know it was Crying Dove. He couldn't tell if she was dead or alive but at that moment, it didn't matter. They had hurt his woman, the one he had come to have more feelings for than any other person in his life. At that moment he came to realize, he loved her.

Making his way back to his horse, he mounted, put the reins in his teeth, lifted the pistol from his holster, and pulled his rifle from the scabbard.

He took a deep breath, and then slapped his feet against the roan's side and felt her leap into a run.

Lucas rode at high speed into the Lakota camp, screaming at the top of his voice, like some demon devil, shooting every brave in sight.

They were so surprised by his attack that within minutes, every male in the small group, lay dead on the ground. The women were screaming and wailing and running to their dead mates – kneeling next to them, singing their death songs.

Lucas stopped next to Crying Dove's body and stepped down. He went to her and immediately cut her bonds. She was breathing heavily and opened her eyes. Her face and lips were swollen and her eyes were purplish, black. Her body was covered with cuts and abrasions.

He took her in his arms and said, "I'm here now."

She smiled the best she could and said in a whisper, "I knew you would come," then took a deep breath and died.

Lucas stood up and looked around. He wanted to kill them all – women, children – all of them for what they'd done. He raised his arms in the air and let out a scream that turned every head to look at him. Several of the women pulled their young close to them.

The gods had sent a crazy person among them and they were filled with fear.

With tears streaming down his face, Lucas told himself, "You are not a heathen, so killing women and children is out of the question. But they need to suffer for what they've done."

First, he got on his horse and drove all but one of their horses, far out away from the camp and watched as they ran into the distant canyon. Next, he rode back into the camp and got down next to the fire in the center of the camp.

Taking a piece of burning wood from the fire, he walked around and set every teepee on fire, not allowing anyone to take anything from any of them.

The women had gathered into a group, with the children standing next to them.

Lucas walked up next to them and asked, "Do any of you speak the white man's language?"

They just stared at him. Next, he spoke in what little Lakota he knew, telling them he would not kill them. If they lived or died it would be the decision of the gods.

And with that, Lucas loaded Crying Dove's body onto the back of the Indian pony, then mounted his horse and left the camp, never looking back, and never knowing that one day, one of the children who survived, would tell the story of what happened, making Lucas Penny, a legend in his own time.

Filled with grief, Lucas rode up next to his cabin and carried Crying Dove inside and laid her on the bed.

Next, he took the bare minimum things he thought he would need, like his guns and ammunition, along with basic things like, a skillet, a coffee pot, a small amount of food, his warm coat. He carried them outside and laid them in a pile, some distance from the cabin.

After taking Crying Dove's horse and the mule, along with a few bags of feed, out to the pile, he went to the barn and got the large container of kerosene.

After pouring some of the kerosene, inside the barn, he went to the cabin and did the same thing.

Lucas built a small fire, then made two torches and threw one inside the cabin and the other inside the barn.

Filled with sadness, Lucas loaded his belongings on the horse and the mule and rode away - two blazing infernos filling the area behind him.

ALSO BY JARED McVAY

Other works by Jared McVay

Jared McVay is an award-winning author who writes, Westerns: A western series: Historical Fiction: Action/Adventure: YA: Children's books: screenplays: teleplays: Short stories, and also does storytelling.

NOVELS:

Western: Clay Brentwood Series- 10 Books:

Historical Fiction: The Legend of Joe, Willy & Red – award winner

Historical Fiction: Silent Runner, Guardian Warrior

Western: Hacker's Raid – award winner

Historical Fiction: Legend of Jubal Courtney

Action/Contemporary - Not on My Mountain – double award winner

JUVENILE FICTION

Brody O'Shea – 3 Books

SCREENPLAYS

The Hobos

Jared & the Warden

Talltree

TELEVISION PILOT SCRIPTS

McClusky [6 episodes] - Drama/Comedy

ACT Acute Care Transport - Drama/Comedy

Melinda: Award winning short story

MEET THE AUTHOR

Jared McVay lives in Oregon where he writes his books, does storytelling, book signings, speaking engagements, and gets in a little fishing from time to time. Before becoming a novelist, Jared was a professional actor – stage, film and television, and a ghostwriter for screenplays.

As a young man he worked as a cowboy, a rodeo clown, a lumberjack, barker for a carnival and a truck driver. During the 1950's he rode the rails as a hobo and during the 80's, a blue water sailor. He spent his military time in the US Navy Sea Bees, where he learned his electrical trade as a power lineman, then spent ten years as a lineman for Kansas Gas & Electric. But it was his love of entertaining people that led him into acting and writing.

Jared has five children, eleven grandchildren, fifteen great grandchildren and four great, great grandchildren.

THANK YOU FOR READING!

If you enjoyed this book, we would appreciate your customer review on your book seller's website or on Goodreads.

Also, we would like for you to know that you can find more great books like this one at www.CreativeTexts.com